BROKEN PROMISES

Book 1.5 of The Fateful Force

Cover Illustration by: Antti Hakosaari
www.artstation.com/haco
Map Illustrations by: Fred Kroner
www.whiskeynink.com
Logo Design by: Elias Dimitakakis
www.creativeinstinct.com.au
Interior Formatting by: Mariana Coello
eBook Design by: Iryna Spica, Spica Book Designs
www.spicabookdesign.com

ISBNs:
978-0-6457636-1-4 (Paperback)
978-0-6457636-0-7 (eBook)

The Fateful Force
Melbourne, Australia
https://thefatefulforce.com

Fateful Force
Book Series

The Tome of Syyx
Broken Promises
Change of Fortune: Prequel Short Story
(This book can be read in any order)
Enemy Within (coming 2024)

Your Free Book is Waiting

A time before grand adventures and ancient evils

Change of Fortune takes place five years before the events of the Epic Fantasy, The Tome of Syyx. It shows Akke as a young street kid, doing what she must to survive in the corrupt city of Newport. Little does she know, that on this fateful day, her life will be forever changed.

Struggling to come to terms with her lot in life, Akke believes beyond hope that she is destined for something greater than to live out her days as a street rat.

So when she is presented with the opportunity to rid herself of the invisible shackles of a corrupt city, Akke does not hesitate to take her fate into her own hands.

But are dreams only for fools and the desperate? And is she just trading one set of shackles for another?

Get a Free copy of the Prequel

Change of Fortune: A Fateful Force Origins Story

https://thefatefulforce.com/the-tome-of-syyx/

Acknowledgements

They say it takes a village to raise a child, and as such a novel is impossible to publish without the help of others. I would like to thank Michelle Balfour and the team at Cascadia Author services, for helping me bring my world to life and holding my hand through the process of achieving my dream of publishing my first novel.

But most of all, I would like to thank Bennett R. Coles, my Creative Editor; without his help, this novel would never have seen the light of day. Thank you, Ben: your guidance and creative input into Broken Promises was invaluable, and the world of Neptos is richer for your ideas and initiatives

Lastly, I would like to thank my loving wife for all her support and allowing me to pull all-nighters playing D&D, which was the spark of inspiration behind my world and novels. Without you none of this would have been possible.

Stavros Saristavros

NEWPORT

POPULATION 100,000

3000 FT

MESSAN
SEA

THE
BLACK SAIL

PUBLIC DOCKS

DOCK ROAD

DOCK SQUARE

TRADE DOCKS

CUTTER'S

SOLDIER'S WAY

SHIPYARD

AKKE'S HIDEOUT

SLUMS

TOWER OF SALT

FISH ROAD

INNER GARDEN

TEMPLE OF LYCOS

PELLIO'S MANOR

GOLDEN GATE

TEMPLE OF MEDEINA

SAFE HOUSE

HIGH ROAD

THE PALACE

SHRINE OF AKUMA

ND MARKET

SHRINE OF IRINI

MAIN ROAD

FARMER'S GATE

TRADE HIGHWAY

RINGS OF GLORY

TEMPLE OF OGUN

THE SHRINE OF VIRTUS

PATH OF GLORY

MAGES ROAD

DAWN'S RAY

FIRST TOWER

TEMPLE OF INANN

H ROAD

PATH OF KNOWLEDGE

PATH OF LIGHT

LIBRARY OF SOFOS

SHRINE OF YAMA

HOUSE OF THE DEAD

LIGHT ROAD

D GATE

NECROPOLIS

Chapter I

"In Newport, the key to survival is simple: stick together."

There was no response from her companion, and Akke listened to her own words drift away on the crisp evening breeze. The only other sound was the gentle rush of water pushed aside by the ship's bow. The silence was broken by the call of a seabird amongst the busy docks that loomed ahead.

For all her years spent living on the streets of Newport, Akke had never seen the city from the water; it made the trading hub look more impressive and inviting than she had ever known it to be. But even this new vantage point did little to lift her sense of dread.

She turned to Ailuros. The panthor's stance was relaxed, his arms folded across his chest and tail swishing idly while his huge green eyes stared out at the port city. The sunset over the tallest towers lit his white fur, casting it in an orange glow, granting the illusion of a warm day. An icy gust ruffled his fur, dispelling that illusion; but if Ailuros felt the chill, he made no sign.

"I thought," he said finally, "that everyone in Newport looked out only for themselves."

"Exactly!" she hissed, surprised at her own vehemence. "Which is why we'll have the advantage."

His gaze flicked down to her, then back up to the city. "You don't have fond memories of this place."

His deep, purring voice always calmed her. She regained her composure banishing her unease and offered him a glance, then looked out at the port again, tugging her hood down low and dipping her head to block the late winter sun.

"It made me who I am," she said simply.

"No, it didn't," Ailuros said with sudden strength.

Akke looked up at him.

"It was merely your first influence," he said. "Fairhaven made you who you are ... And Sanctuary made you the person I admire."

"Rather insightful for a panthor," she teased.

"We are very insightful, witch. Our hunters are considered the greatest in the lands and reading a situation well is the key to survival." He gave her a look. "And I don't want you moping as you show me around this wretched, stinking, glorious place."

She laughed. "I promise to show you a good time. Just remember that we have a mission."

"The girl, yes. What was her name?"

"Ruthia."

Ailuros nodded, a deep rumble in his throat indicating he was lost in thought. Eventually he said simply, "If she's important to you, then she's important to me." He then gazed out at the docks again.

Behind them, the crew of *Fortune's Caress* moved with quiet efficiency, finally hauling down the sails and sliding out her oars along both sides of the merchant galley's broad hull. The trade docks were crowded with vessels, but one sizable berth lay open, and *Fortune's Caress* turned smoothly on the water as its oars splashed to aid the rudder.

Akke scanned the docks, noting the hectic pace of life that was the norm for a busy port. Carts and horses trundled along the cobbled streets, weaving between wooden cranes that swung to offload cargo from ships. People scurried to and fro, loading cargo, barking orders, or running one of the thousands of errands required in a bustling trade centre.

Across from the docks were blocks of large warehouses and workshops, some even three stories tall. The narrow streets between them were already lost in shadow as the sun dipped behind the highest distant spires.

Newport was a colossal city, rumoured to be home to more than a hundred thousand souls. Rising on the low hills in the distance, Akke could just make out the temples, civic buildings, and grand arena that boasted of Newport's prosperity. But that prosperity, she knew, was built on the backs of the nameless wretches scurrying along the docks before her, plus countless other servants, labourers, and petty artisans who kept the gears of progress turning. A part of her would be quite happy to burn the whole place to the ground.

But that was a very small part of her. That was the starving, frightened girl who'd nearly met her end here six summers ago. That wasn't her anymore—even if seeing Newport once again dredged up too many memories.

She pulled her hood off, letting the cold sea breeze wash over the sudden perspiration that had broken out on her skin. Breathing deeply, she fell back on her training and calmed herself, fingering the fine fabric of her cloak and admiring its luxurious fur trim. She was not that girl anymore, she reminded herself. Life on the frontier, fighting orcs, hobgoblins and ... much worse, had changed her. No, she thought with renewed confidence, this was a triumphant return to the city of her birth.

"So where are we going first?" Ailuros asked.

Fortune's Caress was slowly coming alongside the dock. Akke watched as the sailors tossed lines to the workers on the dock and then tied those lines to hawsers that would fix their ship to its berth. The sailors' movements were practiced and efficient; they'd done this a hundred times before. They pointed to Newport and talked excitedly with each other, eyes gleaming in anticipation. Newport with its brothels and taverns was finally a reality.

"We're going to the kind of place where sailors like these often go on their first night ashore." Akke replied.

"Excellent."

"Just a little more dangerous."

"Even better."

Amongst the bustle of the crew Akke noticed the ship's master, Regwald, talking to the ship's officer in charge of the galley's few cannons, and no doubt giving instructions to receive the wizarding guild's representative in Newport. The wizarding guilds of every major nation and city, including Newport, maintained strict regulation on the ownership and use of black powder weapons. Just having them on board spoke of the influence the ship's captain possessed, and of the organisation he represented.

Regwald clapped the officer on the shoulder and strode towards Akke and Ailuros. He cut quite a figure as he crossed the deck, his trim, dark-brown beard and hair laced with silver, his fine tailor-made clothing accentuating his powerful frame that had broadened with age and wealth. Akke admired Regwald for many reasons, but she couldn't quite say that she trusted him. He was a major player in the Network, and that by definition made him untrustworthy.

But then, she thought with a wry grin as she pulled up the hood of her cloak once again, what did that make her?

"Welcome to Newport," Regwald offered. "I'd hesitate to say, 'welcome home,' Akke."

"My luxurious companion insists on seeing every great city in the lands," she replied with a charming smile. "Who am I to deny him?"

Regwald offered Ailuros a slight bow. "Welcome to the show, my friend. May it entertain you."

"If half the stories are true," Ailuros rumbled, "I expect my breath to be taken away."

"Be careful what you wish for," Regwald said with a strange look "Newport is unforgiving."

"Thank you for the offer of accommodation," Akke put in before Ailuros could retort. "We expect to arrive later this evening. Is there an hour after which we'd be turned away?"

"The safehouse is always ready to receive invited guests."

"Thank you."

The deck shifted as *Fortune's Caress* finally settled alongside the jetty. Regwald glanced at the continuing activity of his crew and then smiled at Akke again.

"I take it the information our friends provided you has been useful?"

"Very."

Akke was still getting used to her elevated status in the Network, but she'd flexed her newfound influence by magically *sending* a request for information before *Fortune's Caress* left Fairhaven. Network agents had apparently acted on her request with all speed. She knew this because a document packet had been waiting for her five days ago with a local agent at Land's End, a decent-sized port town en route to Newport. The packet hadn't answered all her questions, but it had given her enough to know where to start.

"So, you have dinner plans already?" Regwald asked.

She nodded. "I'm going to drop in on an old acquaintance."

*

The sun was gone before the gangplank was settled, but neither Akke nor Ailuros were bothered by the darkness as they descended to the dock. The humans around them were busy lighting lamps, and they barely noticed the stealthy half-elf and panthor disappear into the shadows. Akke had no love for the unknown elf who had sired her, but she did appreciate the physical characteristics his blood had gifted her. Her elven eyes bestowed her with night vision, enabling her to see through the gloom of the darkness, and her elven ears allowed her to detect sounds that most other races would struggle to perceive. Here in Newport, they both promised to be particularly useful.

As city folk retreated indoors for the night, traffic died on Dock Road, the major thoroughfare along Newport's large waterfront. Spring was still just a promise, and while the days could be pleasant enough, the temperature plunged once the sun disappeared. That, and the docks were not safe at night.

Akke tightened her cloak around her, but maintained a wide field of vision by resting her fur-trimmed hood on her elaborately braided hair. It was probably too early for real mischief to lurk around every corner—even muggers enjoyed their evening meals—and she took advantage of the quiet streets to wend her way swiftly along the waterfront.

Ailuros trotted along beside her, his huge head swivelling from side to side as his nostrils flared.

"The smells are ... vibrant," he muttered. "Do I detect a hint of dwarf?"

"Likely," she replied. "Every major nation has representatives in Newport to buy and sell. We'll see all sorts here."

"Panthors don't send representatives."

"I said 'major nations.' Your jungle camps and scattered tribes don't really count."

"Why enslave one's family to a ruler in a faraway city? You naked races shun the very freedoms you boast to hold in high esteem."

"And yet, you wanted to come here."

"My curiosity knows no bounds."

She slowed as warehouses gave way to more ramshackle buildings. The waterfront ran three thousand paces north and south along the poorer city wards, of which there were many in Newport. Run-down, wattle-and-daub row houses with shuttered shops, dark doorways, and scattered refuse were a common sight. The occasional bang was echoed by distant dog barks. Firelight from upper-level windows was blocked by tattered curtains drawn against the cold. Most passing by were openly armed but minded their own business as they shuffled along with a sense of purpose.

Akke scanned the scratches hewn into the wooden crossbeam of one building, recognizing the flow of street symbols. The concepts captured within the lines and curves were simple enough for illiterate children to understand, and they'd changed little since her youth. But there was one symbol she'd never seen before: a triangle with a single line extending down from the shortest side: a cleaver. She nodded to herself. The Network had come through.

"You've found something?" Ailuros asked, gazing blankly at the same beam she studied.

"We're in the right part of town. It's under the protection of a guy I once knew. And he should be able to help us find Ruthia, or at least lead us to someone who might."

"And this person is a friend of yours?"

"Well…" She considered for a moment. "I wouldn't go that far, but I used to occasionally do good work for him."

The Network had offered to conduct this meeting on her behalf, but she wanted to take the lead on this mission; Ruthia's safety was too important to leave in the hands of uninvested negotiators.

Ailuros looked down at her. "So why do you think he'll help us?"

"Gold," she answered bluntly. "There isn't much in Newport that's not for sale—for the right price. The information we want isn't likely to get the one providing it killed, so it should be an easy bargain. Plus, we have some history between us."

Alluros looked around the dim street. "So where do we find him?"

She studied the buildings, stilling herself as she listened for the tell-tale sign of ... yes, there: the clink of tankards and laughter over muted voices, half a block inland.

Moving toward a cracked, heavy door through which flickering light escaped, she motioned for Ailuros to follow. "Let me buy you a drink, cat-man."

The door was shut, but it was so loosely hung that its edges glowed with the dim light from the room beyond. Akke gripped the worn metal handle and pushed the door open. She stepped through the doorway into a sudden rush of heat and to be met withthe familiar smells of dodgy meat, boiled vegetables, watery ale, and many unwashed bodies.

The stone-walled room was surprisingly spacious given its low, heavy-beamed ceiling that was blackened at one end from years of smoke curling up from its crumbling hearth. A gnarled woman in far-too revealing clothes tended a cauldron hung over a blazing fire. In the far corner of the room a young man at the wooden bar paused in pulling a pint and observed Akke's entry with curiosity.

Wooden tables filled most of the room, and they were already crowded with a mix of clientele hunkered over their tankards. Off to Akke's left there were some gaming tables crewed by young women, faces hardened beyond their years and dressed to indicate that cards and dice weren't the only games on offer that evening. For a moment Akke imagined Ruthia's face on one of those young girls, but then banished the thought. She had to stay focused.

She stepped forward enough for Ailuros to squeeze his bulk through the door. As the door squeaked shut behind him, she realized that all noise had ceased. Every patron in the tavern stared at them. Many were trying to be surreptitious, but when an entire room falls silent it was hard to blend in. The hooded cloaks she and Ailuros wore were of the finest quality, a fact obvious even in the dim light, and one she expected to draw attention.

Some might call it a risky strategy, but Akke knew how the underbelly of Newport worked. She and Ailuros were strangers—there was no hiding that. If they tried to skulk in unnoticed, they would be perceived as weak or as trying to hide. That would cause an inevitable fight, which she was mostly confident they could survive, but that would bring all kinds of unnecessary damage. Better to draw attention from the outset and bluff their way through.

From the table to her right, barely two paces distant, a hulking human rose to his feet. At his table were four other heavies. Enforcers, most likely. They all straightened in their chairs, but let their boss take the lead, their predatory eyes moving between her and Ailuros.

The hulking man took a step forward. "You boys lost?"

A deep growl rumbled behind her, loud enough to stop the man in his tracks.

Akke flicked off her hood, revealing her elven ears and fine features. A swish of fabric told her Ailuros had done the same. Astonishment rippled through the crowd. The hulking man hesitated, eyes darting between the elf and the panthor, and the aggression in his stance faded. Akke cast her gaze around the entire room.

"I come seeking information," she said in a perfect imitation of the elves who all but ruled Newport, "and I'm prepared to pay a fair price for it. I wish to know the location of an individual called Blade."

Eyes suddenly dropped as people turned back to their tankards. There was a general shuffle of movement and muttered comments that made it clear: no one was in the mood to cooperate. Akke had been expecting this reaction, and thus she wasn't disappointed; Blade himself wasn't the person she expected to find. At least, not yet.

She turned an imperious gaze back to the hulking man who still stood before her. She could tell he was used to being in charge, and his powerful hands had probably taken more than one life. Those hands clenched and unclenched as he tried to size up the situation. She stared him down as he tried to figure out whether these two newcomers were utter fools, or dangerous foes to avoid.

Keeping people off-balance was the key, Akke knew. As soon as they felt they understood a situation, they might be tempted to do something they'd regret.

Why, he was desperately trying to puzzle out as he withered under her gaze, was an elf in this part of town? In his mind, the fairies never sullied themselves amongst the lesser races—certainly never at night and with only a single bodyguard.

She stepped toward him, putting him off-balance even more. "Attacking a noble-born carries with it severe consequences," she said quietly, still holding his gaze. "And with so many witnesses, someone will surely rat you out when the authorities descend upon this place."

Another swish of Ailuros' cloak was followed by the soft thump of his spear butt against the floor.

"That is," she concluded with a wicked smile, "assuming my cat doesn't get you first."

From across the room, the young barkeep suddenly called out, "Milady! There's no one named Blade here, but perhaps I could offer you and your companion a drink."

He'd raised his hand as if to capture her attention, but that hand moved with quick, subtle gestures that Akke recognized as thieves' cant. He was telling the hulking man to back off, and that he would handle the situation.

As the man heavily retook his seat and made a point of turning away to grasp his ale, Akke stepped into the depths of the tavern. The men and women at the gaming tables started their games up again and, as Akke weaved between the other patrons, the general hubbub of the room slowly returned to normal.

She sidled up to the bar, dropping a couple of iron pigs on the worn counter. Ailuros appeared beside her and stood half-turned to keep an eye on the room.

"What can I get you, milady?" the barkeep asked, a curious smile dancing on his lips.

"Ailuros! what can I get the panthor who has everything?" she asked, keeping her eyes on the young human—he so looked familiar.

"Give me what they're all drinking." He gestured at the crowd.

In high society a bodyguard would never indulge while on duty, but here in the gutter it would seem odd if he didn't. Drunken guards were a constant threat in Akke's youth, and she knew that if the tavern patrons saw the panthor down a few, they'd be even more wary of him.

The barkeep produced a mug of ale and set it down

in front of Ailuros, but his eyes stayed on her. "Akke?" he asked finally in a tone of disbelief.

Recognition finally dawned, and Akke once again reflected on how the Network had come through; their information had led her right to her target. He was just a few years older than her; last time she'd seen him he'd been barely an adult, vying for dominance on the petty mole hill that was his sordid corner of Newport. He'd grown up, filled out, and carried a few more scars, but he still had that same, boyish charm.

"Cutter." She smiled, remembering the nickname he'd tried so hard to get everyone to call him.

He chuckled, dropping his eyes momentarily. "In here it's just Zel."

Meaning he led a double life, moonlighting as a barkeep. But his little display with the thieves' cant and getting a bunch of heavies to back down meant his bid for power had been successful.

"And Blade? Did I get *his* name right?"

"Yeah." Zel raised his eyes again, holding hers, his expression serious. "But Blade hasn't been seen in this part of town for years."

Meaning Zel and Blade weren't on the same crew and were likely rivals, which tied in with what the Network had reported to her about the area. This made the situation delicate: a gang giving up information on their rival could lead to bloodshed. But she was confident the risk was nothing a bit of coin couldn't solve.

Ailuros suddenly slammed the empty tankard on the table. "Barkeep," he growled, "is this actually urine, or does it just taste like it?"

"It's a local favourite."

"Pah!" The panthor pointed at the fancier of the two draw-handles behind the bar. "What about this one? Is it quality?"

"Ah, that's our finest brew. But it costs a copper a cup."

Akke glanced around at the bar. The arrival of two mysterious strangers had already lost the interest of the patrons and keeping up a friendly banter with Zel would only put them more at ease. She placed a copper on the counter. Zel dutifully drew a new pint and handed it to Akke.

"So," Akke said, leaning in and offering Zel a charming smile, "you know where I can find Blade?"

"Hmm ..." he scratched his chin, making a great show of thinking. "Like I said, haven't seen him in years."

She slid another copper on the bar.

He looked down at the coin with disappointment. "I'm pretty sure he's still in the city, but I really don't know where."

This time she produced a silver eagle but kept it in her hand.

"Ohhh, wait," he said. "Yes, I remember. He runs a crew in the Northern Docks."

She closed her hand around the eagle. "I already knew that, Zel. Try again."

The Network had told her that much, but Blade's precise movements were unknown. It seemed his life as a crime boss was filled with paranoia, and he never stayed in one location for too long.

Zel grinned at her. "He keeps a couple of places well

north of Main Road."

She opened her hand. He dragged his fingers across her palm to retrieve the silver eagle.

"How do I know which place he's staying at?" she asked.

A spray of beer across the bar made her wince. Zel's eyes went wide as he grabbed a cloth to wipe down the surface.

"This is exactly the same as the other beer!" Ailuros exclaimed.

"No, sir," Zel replied quickly, gesturing to the fancier pull handle. "You saw me draw it myself from this fine handle."

Ailuros made to look over the bar. "And do both pull from the same keg?"

Zel deftly tossed the cloth down beneath the counter, probably covering up the keg. "That's impossible! I wouldn't even know how to do something like that."

Akke tossed a couple more coppers on the bar. "Perhaps another drink will make this right?"

"At least!" Ailuros declared.

Zel drew another cup and handed it over before setting both his elbows on the bar and leaning toward Akke. "Now, where were we?"

She treated him to a coy smile. "You were going to tell me which of Blade's places he's staying in tonight."

"I wouldn't have the foggiest idea."

Akke dropped her smile. She produced another pair of silver eagles, holding them in her hand as she fixed Zel with hard eyes.

Zel kept his smile in place, but she could tell he sensed the shift in mood. "I hear he favours one of the north side warehouses off Dock Road, near Potter Street and Reaver's Way." He hesitated, but before Akke could reprimand him he continued. "I don't know which one, exactly, but he runs a crew of kids as advance look-outs. If you see them, you're in the right place."

"You sure?"

"That's what I hear."

She put the eagles on the bar. "You better not be playing me."

His hand reached out to touch hers. Akke felt Ailuros tense beside her, but she knew there was no malice in Zel.

Zel leant toward her. "He's not the same guy you knew," Zel said, voice low.

"I expect he's exactly the same guy I knew," she whispered back. "Just fatter and with more goons."

A quiet chuckle escaped his lips. For the first time in the conversation his guard came down, and for a second she saw the boy she'd once known. "In some ways you've hardly changed," he said softly. "You were a cute little thing back in the day. But, Akke ... you are truly beautiful now."

She let her face light up. "Thanks."

"What kind of mess are you in that you need to find Blade?"

She considered for a moment. Revealing information always carried a risk, and usually required a cost. But Zel seemed to be playing the trust-me card, and her mission wasn't really a secret.

"I'm looking for an old friend. Ruthia."

He frowned in thought, then shook his head.

"She was much younger than me, usually worked the Grand Marketplace as a beggar. Curly, yellow hair."

His face lit up in faint recognition and he nodded.

"Do you know where she is?"

"Sorry." He sighed. "I really don't. But I'm pretty focused down here at the docks. If she's still working the markets I wouldn't hear. But ..."

Akke set down yet another copper.

"When one of us goes missing or gets into trouble, word spreads. I haven't heard about anything bad happening to someone named Ruthia."

Relief flooded through Akke, almost enough to overwhelm her well-practiced smile. The higher-ups of the city might not take notice, but rumours did spread among the underbelly of the city whenever a street kid was punished or disappeared. There was no telling what had happened to Ruthia in the past six years, but that small statement reassured her that it wasn't a truly terrible fate.

At least she hoped.

"Then I guess," she said, "I need to talk to Blade. Tonight."

Zel stared at her, a sad smile playing across his features. He looked down at the considerable coin he had already netted during this little negotiation and his eyes softened again.

He reached out gently one last time, taking her by the elbow and pulling his lips close to her ear. "This one is free: right after you disappeared, things got strange. That fat merchant prince, Pellio, turned the streets upside-down looking for you." His eyes were clouded with worry. "If he finds out you're back in town, no fancy clothes, pointed ears, or panthor bodyguard will keep you safe."

"Well, then," she whispered back, "you're the only one in here who knows my name. Please keep it that way." She gave him a quick kiss on the cheek and turned to leave.

She had made the right choice, seeking out Cutter.

CHAPTER 2

The night was growing cold and Akke was thankful for her cloak as she and Ailuros stalked the shadows in complete silence. The rising moon cast a silvery glow along the teetering buildings to her left, and her elven eyesight confirmed that the dark warehouses to her right were still.

Ailuros followed a few steps behind, hood drawn up, not because of the cold, but to hide his features. There were very few people about, but it only took one to report a panthor on the prowl. There were times to be flamboyant, Akke knew, but this wasn't one of them.

They'd already sighted their mark: a young lad pretending to scavenge through some refuge. This late at night, in this part of town, either the child was a fool or under someone's protection. Following Cutter's information, Akke guessed it was the latter. They must be close.

Akke glanced at Ailuros and nodded toward the child. The panthor slipped into the darkness while Akke maintained watch for any secondary sentries.

As silently as he left, Ailuros returned bare moments later, the small child in his embrace, his furry hand covering the lad's mouth to prevent any outbursts, and the lad's eyes staring out over the fur in pure terror. Ailuros placed the lad gently on the ground, keeping his paw pressed firmly for silence.

Akke crouched down for a closer look, keeping her own face hidden in the shadows of her cloak. Beneath the filth, Akke was surprised to see that the 'lad' was actually a young girl, no more than ten summers. Frightened, dirty, and dishevelled, but looking surprisingly well-fed.

"There's no need to scream," Akke whispered reassuringly, but in the heavy local accent of the Newport lower class. "We just have some questions. If you answer truthfully, no harm will come to you."

She would never hurt a child, of course, but this little girl didn't know that. The girl nodded, fighting down her panic.

"Which warehouse is Blade in?"

The girl's eyes flicked left and right, her breathing quick under Ailuros' paw.

Akke produced a copper coin, more than this child would see in a week begging on the streets. The child's eyes fixed on it, visibly relaxing enough that Ailuros removed his hand from her mouth.

"Please don't let the lion eat me," the girl squeaked.

Akke raised her free hand to quell the protest growing in Ailuros' throat.

"Just tell us where Blade is, and I promise you won't be harmed."

"The warehouse next to the Black Sail," came the whisper. "Thirty paces down Dock Road and right on Reaver's Way."

Akke knew the child was telling the truth. She was intimately familiar with the law of the streets: give false info for real coin, and you'd could very likely end up dead—or worse. She'd been in the exact same position as this young waif many years ago.

She fished out another copper and the child's eyes lit up. She nodded to Ailuros, who let the young girl go.

Akke leant in one final time. "Go quietly, tell no one about us, and lay low for a day."

The child gripped the coins to her chest and slid away in the opposite direction.

"Lions," Ailuros growled, "are lazy, stupid beasts. Did I call her a baboon?"

"You've called others worse."

"Fair enough, witch."

*

Akke peeked around the corner of the dark intersection. Across Reaver's Way was the quiet frontage of the Black Sail, the tavern's windows dark and its common room shut for the night. Twenty paces further, she saw an armed man standing sullenly in front of a pair of wide doors. Light glowed from behind him, and a single flicker suggested someone moving inside. An open window just below the peaked roof also glowed. Akke watched for a long moment and then spotted a moving figure above it— another sentry, likely with a crossbow.

Ailuros pressed in beside her, his feline eyes assessing the situation. "Two guards," he concluded. "Easy enough. I'll take the one by the door if you can silence the one on the roof."

She'd been thinking the same thing and merely nodded. Ailuros slunk back, crossed the road behind her, and then padded silently across the intersection. Even Akke could barely see him and had no worries about the sentry by the door, who was clearly human by the way he stared blankly into the darkness. Within moments Ailuros stalked along the front of the warehouse to within striking range.

Akke spotted the guard on the roof and breathed deeply, summoning her magic. Just as Ailuros wrapped his arms around the door guard's neck in a choking vice, Akke reached out her arms and pushed out a single command.

Sleep.

Within a heartbeat, both guards were silently dispatched. There was a soft thump as the roof sentry collapsed, barely audible over Akke's own footsteps as she dashed across the street to where Ailuros was gently laying down his victim. The human was still breathing, she noted.

"Nice move," she whispered.

"Something our dear friend Osho taught me," he muttered.

She nodded curtly, pushing away a sudden surge of sadness. Osho was perhaps the finest individual she'd ever known but thinking about him only reminded of her own many, many failings. Rescuing Ruthia was one way she intended to balance that ledger. Osho would no doubt approve but thinking about him would distract her from the mission.

It was much easier to focus on the here and now.

She peeked through the crack around one of the warehouse doors. The interior space was cleared in the centre, and she could see at least four people. After listening for a few moments, she made out two distinct voices, jockeying back and forth in what was clearly a negotiation. But not a friendly one: one voice took on more and more of an edge while the other began to quail in fear.

"Sounds like Blade is doing some late-night business," she whispered.

"Do you want to crash the party?" Ailuros asked.

"No. Whoever the other person is, we have no quarrel with them. We'll let them finish, then I'll re-introduce myself. Can you get up to that window on the roof?"

"Can a dwarf guzzle a pony keg?"

"Get up there and tie the sentry up. We might be here for a while. We don't want him waking and causing trouble before we finish our business. Then get inside, find a perch, and stay hidden."

"And you?"

"I'll take care of the one down here, then walk right in the front door."

"Do you expect this Blade to be willing to talk?"

She hesitated. In all honesty, she had no idea what to expect. Blade had always been a bully, but bullies were commonplace here. That wasn't likely to have changed in the years since she'd known him, but she hesitated, thinking of Cutter's warning.

"No. So if not, we'll have to convince him."

"Understood."

Ailuros retreated a few steps, shed his cloak, then pounced upward. His claws dug into the wooden wall, and he scampered silently upward.

Akke turned to the guard Ailuros had dispatched, tying his wrists and gagging him before returning her attention to the drama inside. Then, realizing by the satisfied tone of the aggressor that the negotiations had concluded, she stepped back, just as movement came toward her.

One of the warehouse doors slid open with a squeal, ejecting a man who huddled his arms around himself against the sudden cold. He shuffled away into the night, not glancing up even once.

"Hey," came a deep voice from within, "shut that door!"

Akke slipped through the opening, scanning left and right for any guards just inside the entrance. A powerful man with a club at his hip loitered barely a pace to her left, and Akke's hand was up before he could do more than widen his eyes in surprise.

Sleep.

It took considerable effort to put someone that large to sleep, but he crumpled to the ground. Akke stepped clear, ensured her hood was drawn fully forward, and walked slowly into the warehouse.

She reminded herself that this was already her second spell; she could only cast a limited number per day. Two sleep spells in short order left her feeling drained, and she needed all her remaining reserves to deal with unforeseen developments.

For all her Network intelligence, and all her skill at knowing people, there was honestly no telling how Blade would react to her presence. The last time they saw each other, he'd made unsavoury demands of her body as payment for working for him, and she'd threated to kill him in his sleep.

She checked her daggers and calmly reminded

herself she still had a couple more tricks up her sleeve.

The floor was hard-packed dirt, with curved grooves that revealed where heavily laden carts had recently passed. Lanterns hung from a half-dozen posts, bathing the space with warm light. The two-storey room was piled high with crates on all sides, but a central area remained clear. There, a burly man sat on a single crate. He was dressed in quality clothes—nothing too expensive, but clearly crafted by a skilled hand. He looked up in surprise, surprise that faded quickly into mild interest.

No fear, Akke noted.

She also noted a man leaning with crossed arms against the stack of crates to her right, and another with a hand on his sword to her left. And, almost lost among the wind whispering through the cracks in the wooden walls, she heard the creak of a rafter high above her.

The well-dressed man in the centre stood slowly, making a show of rolling his shoulders as he sized her up. "A mysterious stranger enters my warehouse," he mused. "Should I be frightened, or intrigued?"

Blade hadn't aged as well as Zel. While the barkeep still had the glow of youth about him, Blade was looking worn. His face was craggy beneath his scratchy beard, and under his shock of messy hair she could see half an earlobe missing. He limped ever-so-slightly as he stepped clear of the crate, favouring his left leg. Even so, he moved with power and confidence.

"You could be rich," she said with her fake elven accent. "All you need to do is answer my question correctly."

"I'm already rich," he said, stretching his arms out to encompass the warehouse. "And what possible question could one of the fair folk have for me?"

"I'm looking for a girl."

"Who isn't?" Blade interrupted, eliciting rough laughter from his goons.

"A very specific girl." Akke stepped forward to close the distance with him. "With golden hair. Name of Ruthia."

Blade sidestepped, clearing the crate and keeping some distance between them. His eyes narrowed at the name, and both his hands lifted slightly from his sides, two fingers flicking. "Why would I know that? I'm just a simple man making his way in life."

One of the goons straightened and left his perch against the wall of crates. The other shuffled into a flanking position.

"Don't insult me. You're the local power in these parts—I'm sure nothing escapes your notice." Akke pulled out a gold crown and tossed it on the ground between them.

He eyed the coin. Even with all the illegal business he conducted, a crown was no insignificant sum. Over a month's salary for a labourer.

He assessed her anew, then grinned. "If you have one of those, you probably have more."

"Give me Ruthia and you can have another."

"Or," he said, "I could just take your entire purse right now."

"This doesn't have to go this way, Blade," Akke warned. "Just tell me where Ruthia is, and we can remain friends."

"I don't know any elves," he said with sudden venom. "And I don't have any friends."

They had her surrounded. Time to knock them off-balance. She dropped her cloak to the ground. Her deep-blue, tailored gambeson armour betrayed her preparedness for trouble. She shifted her weight and placed hands on the daggers at her hip. She lifted her chin, giving him a clear look at her face.

"Don't be so sure, Razir."

It was his childhood name. Uttering it had exactly the effect she expected. He stared at her in sudden confusion. His lips parted, but no sound came out.

She stepped closer, keeping his goons in her peripheral as she locked eyes with him. "You've come a long way," she said with a sly smile, "but I could take you much, much further."

The look of shock crossing his face as recognition suddenly dawned on him was priceless. Akke's guess was correct: Blade hadn't changed at all. He was still the same piece of crap she remembered.

"You!" His eyes went hard as steel as he flicked his fingers. The goons attacked.

Blade strode forward, murder in his eyes as he reached for his own daggers. But his hands had barely reached his belt when Ailuros pounced, dropping from his perch in the rafters with a deafening roar.

Blade collapsed under the weight of the panthor, hitting the ground hard. Ailuros was already in the air again, the butt of his spear cracking across the skull of the goon to Akke's left. The man crumpled to the dirt.

To his credit, the other goon didn't freeze in shock at the sudden attacks: he got his club up and was moving to the offensive. Akke channelled her magic again, filling the space behind the goon with a sudden clamour of noise, as if half-a-dozen soldiers had just charged in.

The goon spun in surprise, club up to defend against the illusory ambush. Akke lunged forward, striking the back of his skull with her dagger hilt. He collapsed, unconscious, and his club clattered to the floor.

The *minor illusion* was a simple spell. Even so it took more of Akke's energy, and she had to clear her head.

Blade cursed in fury as he tried pulling himself up to his hands and knees, but Ailuros pounced, pinning Blade to the floor once again. The panthor gripped Blade's hair and pulled his face up. The human snarled, but otherwise didn't move. Akke crouched down next to him.

"*Blade...*" She let the name hang in the air. "This doesn't have to end badly. Just tell me where Ruthia is, and you'll never see me again."

He glared at her. "Why do you want to know?"

She sighed, lowering one of her daggers to his throat. "I let you go last time. Don't make me reconsider that decision."

"You think you can waltz in here, all fancy-like, and tell me what to do?"

"Yeah..." She let that simple statement hang. "It seems I can."

"I don't know where your little bitch is."

"Ailuros, jog his memory."

The panthor slammed Blade's face into the hard-packed floor. When he pulled it up, blood mixed with the dirt. Blade spat.

"You do know where she is," Akke said coldly. "And

you're going to tell me."

"She's beyond your reach."

"You mean she's beyond yours. Just tell me."

He spat again.

"Ailuros, claws."

Blade hissed in pain as twenty tiny daggers punched into his skin. "Okay! Okay! She's part of the Serpent gang!"

Akke searched her memory. The Serpents had been a particularly nasty group of enforcers in her youth. They worked out of the eastern market district, providing muscle for some of the less-savoury merchants in town.

"What does she do with the Serpents?"

"I don't know. Cooks and cleans, probably—a kid like her isn't good for much else."

"I need you to introduce me to the Serpents."

"Not a chance. Their boss and me don't exactly see eye to eye."

"I'm sure you could make an exception."

"Akke," his voice took on a softly exasperated tone, "if I walk in there, they'll kill me before I can open my mouth. They're part of the Guild now. I can't touch 'em."

She sensed no deception, and her heart whirled at this revelation. Elation that Ruthia was alive mixed with consternation that things had just become more complicated.

The Serpents had no affiliation with the Network, so she couldn't rely on help from her allies. And if they were under the protection of the Thieves' Guild, just strolling in was out of the question. But there were always methods to gain the right introduction.

They'd learned all they could, and Blade's goons would be back on their feet soon. Three spells in one day was more than she'd cast in months, and it was dulling her senses. Her magic was nearly dry, and she didn't want to tempt fate.

"If you go in there," Blade spat, "You'll end up dead. Maybe your girl too. And I'll laugh for the rest of the year."

Anger flared, and her dagger pressed against the skin of his neck. But her memory flickered back to the young girl she and Ailuros had questioned, and how she'd appeared surprisingly well-fed. Blade might be a piece of crap, but it looked like he took care of his crew. Killing him would create a power vacuum, and that young girl might end up with an even worse master: this was Newport, after all.

"Enjoy the crown." She reached into her purse and tossed a second gold coin on the ground. "And here's another to forget you ever saw me."

Blade was a scumbag, but hardly the worst scumbag in history. She stood, staring down at him as he assessed her with his furious eyes. "No hard feelings, Blade."

She turned, walking past the stirring goons. "By the way, two of your guards are tied up outside, and it's getting cold out there."

She heard Blade grunt in pain as Ailuros leapt off him and landed at her side, spear in hand. Together they strolled out of the warehouse, maintaining a forced casualness until they entered the shadows of the street.

"Let's get out of here," she whispered.

Chapter 3

The next morning brought with it clear skies and new warmth. Akke leaned back in her bath with a sigh as the golden rays of sunlight shone down on her face. She hadn't come to Newport looking for creature comforts, but after her time out on the frontier she couldn't deny that it was nice to be back in civilization. The bath water was hot and soapy, her bed last night had been soft and luxurious, and the house's servants had been polite and attentive. Arching back in a stretch that reached all the way to her toes, she sighed again.

Having earned a senior position in the Network, she was beginning to appreciate why people like Regwald stayed in the business for so long: life was comfortable at the top. This entire manor house was owned by the Network. It perched at the edge of the wealthiest district in the city, Light Town—named so for its magical lights that illuminated the street at night.

The manor itself was surrounded by high walls, which were in turn guarded by magical wards and discreet watchers. But the front gates were a decoy; the actual entrance was via an ordinary-looking house a block away that was connected to an underground tunnel. Akke felt safe here, and her sleep last night had been restful.

She cast her eyes around the bathing chamber: stone arches stretched up from pillars and half-walls that divided it into several sections. The artistry of the carving was exquisite, and each painted dome in the ceiling portrayed a scene of idyllic bliss. From behind one of the half-walls, she could hear Ailuros splashing in his own bath; from the sounds of it, he was climbing out of the tub.

He rose into view, tall enough that he was head and shoulders above the half-wall that separated them. His white fur was slick against his powerful torso as he ran a paw over his wet ears.

He stopped, suddenly noticing her gaze. "Beholding true magnificence?" he purred.

She rolled in the tub, leaning both her elbows on the edge as she examined him further. The dripping fur was not flattering. "You look like a drowned rat," she decided.

"If you were a female panthor, you'd probably be presenting by now," he said with a huff. "You naked races have no appreciation for true beauty."

"Oh, really?" Staying on her knees, Akke lifted her arms and shoulders high out of the water, leaning against the high tub just enough to preserve her modesty. Water and soap dripped off her skin, and the sudden rush of cold air made her skin tingle.

"Smooth, silky skin," she said as she stretched luxuriantly, "is true beauty."

His large, green eyes scanned her leisurely. "You look like a kitten."

"I'll take that," she said with a satisfied smile.

"A newborn, hairless, helpless kitten still dripping with afterbirth."

She dropped her arms to lean against the rim of the tub. "What?"

Ailuros grabbed a towel and started rubbing his fur to dry it. "Bare skin," he muttered, "is utterly unattractive. I pity you. Now, dwarven men and their hairy women ... They have some style."

Akke tried to frown, but a laugh rumbled up her throat. She knew he was lying, at least somewhat.

He disappeared into his chambers, and Akke reluctantly climbed out of her own bath, wrapping herself in a towel as she strolled into the rooms assigned to her.

Sunlight streamed in through the broad window, revealing her clothing and armour from last night, now cleaned and neatly placed at the foot of her poster bed. She slipped into her soft leggings and shirt before donning her gambeson tunic, leaving it unfastened. She was content to pad around in bare feet on the heated floors. How they managed to channel steam under the tiles still amazed her.

A few minutes seated by the mirror with a silver brush and her long, auburn hair was cascading smoothly past her shoulders. She took a final second to examine the woman looking back at her in the reflection and decided that she liked what she saw.

A knock on the far side of the room was followed by the slight creak of hinges as the door cracked open. "Mistress," came a young voice, "may I bring you breakfast?"

"Yes, please," she replied, standing from the mirror.

A much deeper voice called from the corridor. "And are you up for guests?"

Intrigued, she crossed the room and sat down at the round, wooden table. "Of course," she replied.

The serving boy carried a tray of breakfast in and set it down on the table, bowing slightly before retreating past the older man who entered. The man was dressed in simple, high-quality clothes, and his expression was warm under a beard that had gone mostly grey. He'd definitely aged in the past six years, and Akke couldn't help but wonder if things in Newport were far worse than they seemed.

She determinedly kept her seat as he approached, his gaze taking in the view of the city beyond before settling on her. Even though they'd been reunited last evening upon arriving at the manor, she still fought down a flurry of emotions upon seeing his face.

"Good morning, Akke."

"Good morning, Patrick."

This was the man who had saved her from destitution and, in all likelihood, slavery. The man who had seen something in a starving street waif and given her the greatest gift anyone could receive: empowerment. She didn't like owing anything to anyone, but even years later she could hardly deny the truth. She owed him *everything*.

"Please," she said, gesturing to the second chair, "join me."

"Are your chambers to your satisfaction?" he asked, pouring them both some tea.

"Do you think I'm some pampered court flower who travels by sedan chair?" she retorted with a smile. "I've spent most of the last year sleeping on the ground. This is lovely."

"Good. But I gather you won't be staying long."

"Just long enough to rescue Ruthia." She meant to stop there, but just couldn't let the moment pass. "And finish what should have been done six years ago."

If Patrick sensed the sudden hostility he gave no

indication, buttering a slice of toast before adding a dollop of jam.

Akke knew the Network well enough now to understand that the mission always trumped the individual. The greater good of the organisation was the goal, not any one person's fate or desires. It was why when Patrick rescued her, she'd had to leave Ruthia behind, despite promising to look out for the girl. She'd accepted that for years, but Ailuros and her dear friends from Sanctuary had shown her another way: sometimes the individual mattered more than any organization.

Osho had mattered. Zom, another dear friend, mattered. And if a half-orc could overcome his bestial instincts and a lifetime of pain to become a better man, Akke could take a few risks to right an old wrong here in Newport. The Network might not consider Ruthia to be of any value, but that wasn't going to stop Akke from fixing a broken promise.

"So, the Serpent gang is beyond our influence?" she asked.

"Yes. A few incidents in recent years have painted the Network in a bad light in some quarters of the city. We don't really care, frankly, and it's not worth the effort to fix. But it does make your request more difficult."

"All I need is a half-dozen willing people. We can be in and out in less than a bell."

Or just Zom, she thought. That half-orc was a one-man wrecking machine.

"And such a brazen attack," Patrick countered calmly, "would bring even further trouble to us—the kind that *we do* care about."

"How did the Serpents get tied to the Thieves' Guild, anyway? I thought they were just thugs."

"The Guild always appreciates new muscle. But more than that, they appreciate control. Every petty gang under their sway means another section of the city they own."

"And how are we situated with the Guild?"

Patrick took a tiny bite and swallowed. "They consider us their primary rival."

"So, petitioning the Guild for a goodwill gesture isn't going to work."

"Not without the proper introduction." He took another bite as she waited patiently. "And of course, I can arrange that for you."

"Thank you." She sipped her tea.

He finished his toast. "You really should eat something—it'll get cold."

"What can you arrange for me?" she prompted with a smile.

"There's an influential man who appreciates the special services the Network can provide, one who excels at keeping all doors in this city open, including those to the Guild. And word has spread of your heroics over the winter. He's expressed interest in meeting the 'god-slayer.'"

"It was a warlock priest, actually, not a god. I don't want to overstate the incident."

Or more accurately, she hated bringing up the memory of the cost of destroying Aramon. Her actions had saved the day, but only at the expense of Osho's life.

Ailuros would be furious if he knew how much this tortured her. Osho had been as close to him as anyone else, and he'd died an honourable warrior's death, protecting his friends. Or so Ailuros often reminded her. She hated when the silly cat was right.

Patrick offered an elaborate shrug, pretending not to notice Akke's sudden change in mood. "Tales from the frontier are rarely heard this far east unless they're truly remarkable. Sometimes an embellishment or two is required to give the story ... the proper legs."

"So long as he isn't going to want some demonstration of my god-slaying power."

"No. He's a realist when it comes to battling the dark forces of this world, and I think you've earned his respect. At least, enough that he's willing to meet you."

A sudden thought struck her. "It isn't Pellio, is it? I don't think I earned his respect."

Patrick laughed. "No, my dear, you most certainly did not. And he's never forgotten that a street urchin somehow broke into his private chambers—security around his home has been tripled ever since. He even sends out punisher squads against any of the homeless seen near his concerns. The man is paranoid." Patrick's humour suddenly faded. "And dangerous. It's not Pellio I'm sending you to, and I'd advise you to stay as far away from him as possible."

"Like I said, I'm not staying in Newport long. I get my friend. I get out of here."

Patrick nodded.

"So, who am I meeting?"

"Do you recall a merchant company called Costa's Curios?"

Akke blinked in surprise. "Of course." Costa's Curios was an institution in Newport: a famous adventuring band of merchants. But that wasn't all. Akke had spied on them—for Blade, of all people—six years ago. It was her last successful job before she'd fled Newport.

"Costa himself would like to meet you."

CHAPTER 4

Akke shifted in her seat as the coach bounced over another loose cobblestone. The velvet curtains on either side swung in a drunken dance as the entire compartment rocked, allowing the fading sun to briefly pierce the carriage's dim interior.

Ailuros pressed both paws down on his seat; she was pretty sure she saw his claws digging into the wood.

"You know," she said, adjusting the fur stole around her bare shoulders, "when I was a kid, I used to watch these carriages thunder by. I imagined the wealthy people inside them, sitting comfortably in their soft luxury."

"Perhaps we should have walked," Ailuros sniffed, snarling involuntarily as the compartment bucked again. "I'd hate to destroy your childhood illusions."

"It's all right," she replied, peeking out through the curtains at the busy Newport streets rushing by. "I have no illusions left, about anything."

"And yet we continue to play the game."

"Of course." She flashed him a genuine smile. "We're doing something real, right under the noses of all these ignorant fops."

Ailuros nodded.

He looked splendid in his rich green tunic, black

leggings, knee-high boots, and feathered hat. She'd watched his eyes light up when he'd seen the wardrobe she'd selected for him, and he now wore the ensemble with easy confidence. His usual spear had no place where they were going, but she hoped his sheer size and his menacing countenance would be deterrent enough.

The carriage slowed to a halt. When the door opened, Akke shifted to her feet and climbed down the rickety steps, realizing anew how her dress, although the height of fashion, gave her exquisite freedom of movement. The silk cloth hugged her figure to just below the waist, where it billowed out to cascade around her legs. Her shoulders were bare, as the dress narrowed below her shoulders to mere strips that met in a fabric collar around her neck.

Her shoes tapped down on the cobbles, and she adjusted the fur stole over her shoulders against the sudden chill. The late afternoon sun was low in the sky, and the breeze carried a final kiss of winter.

Down the long street that the carriage had just ascended, Akke could see most of Newport stretching out before her. The grander buildings of Light Town were to the northwest, and in the distance, she could make out the tall merchant building surrounding the Grand Market. The low mass of shops, warehouses, and homes spread all the way to the harbour where sailing ships dotted the deep blue of the bay.

Ailuros appeared next to her, the breeze rustling his fur. "So many people, all clustered together. For warmth? For safety?"

"For those who have the choice," she replied, "it's wealth. For everyone else, it's survival."

"It leaves me almost speechless."

"A rare thing indeed."

The breeze tugged at the heavy, jewelled earrings that dangled from her ears, and she reached up to adjust the tiny gold chain that stretched from the earring to the clip against her pointed upper earlobe. Just above that, a golden tiara nestled firmly in her intricately coiled hair, which swept up to reveal her slender neck beneath the fur.

Ailuros gave her an approving nod. "You look magnificent, witch."

Akke smiled at the genuine compliment.

They then turned to survey the building where their carriage had stopped. It was a large and well-kept stone edifice, perhaps seven or eight men tall. There was no sign proclaiming what awaited them inside, but the quality of patrons presenting themselves at the single, iron door betrayed its purpose. The Palace of Pleasure, or simply the Palace, was the grandest gambling hall in all of Newport. Only the wealthiest or most connected of patrons were permitted within its domain. A pair of guards in gentleman's clothes checked patrons' invitations and quietly ushered them through the door.

"You ready, witch?"

"Let's make our presence known," she said, motioning for him to follow. She strolled up to the steps with feigned confidence, noting the alert eyes in the pair of men watching the door. She sensed Ailuros tense behind her as he readied himself for an ambush.

"The door, gentlemen, if you please," she said in a crisp accent that imitated the elves of Fairhaven. "I'm catching a chill out here."

One of the men extended his hand. "Your invitation,

milady," he replied.

Akke snapped her hand back expectantly. As planned, Ailuros placed an envelope into it. She then offered the envelope to the man. He took it, flicked it open, and pulled out the card inside. It was, she knew, a genuine invitation procured for her by the Network.

The man handed it back to her with a sudden smile and he straightened. "Welcome, Lady Toriel," he said, opening the door, "to the Palace of Pleasure."

Akke stepped through the stone arch, appreciating the warmth and incense that rushed over her. The corridor extended a few strides before turning sharply to the left, opening up to reveal a magnificent sight.

The Palace was a feast for the eyes. Brightly coloured murals stretched across sections of wall, and tall, narrow braziers provided modest warmth throughout. Magical lamp posts cast gentle light at regular intervals in the walkways between the gaming tables so that the lavishly dressed patrons could move with easy purpose across the floor. Crowds thronged around other patrons playing elaborate games of chance and, down every side of the vast room, long tables strained under the weight of exquisite food.

Akke strolled along the perfectly cut marble tiles into the gaming hall. A gorgeous young man appeared before Akke, offering a tray with two flutes of chilled wine. He was blond and sharp-featured, and probably younger than her, for his plunging neckline revealed baby-smooth skin on his muscular, hairless chest. His full lips didn't move as he offered the drinks, but his eyes spoke volumes. Everything in here, it seemed, was available for a price.

Akke took one of the drinks and turned away,

indicating her disinterest in anything else he was offering. A low growl behind her indicated that Ailuros had refused the second glass.

Akke took a slow sip, trying to quell the anxiety in her stomach. High society gatherings such as this were a long way from the frontier, and even longer from the street urchin she had been. But she had to keep moving and keep up the charade if she was going to find Costa and her way into an introduction to the Thieves' Guild.

She'd barely taken ten steps when a stunning young woman approached, lustrous black hair bouncing around her shoulders as she politely greeted the pair and wished them a pleasant evening. Her outfit was at least as revealing as the young man's, displaying her ample cleavage and shapely legs. Her dark eyes smouldered at Akke, betraying her intentions behind the phrase "a pleasant evening."

Akke gave a polite nod and continued walking, hearing another low growl behind her. It was going to be tough for Ailuros to maintain the role of sober, celibate bodyguard for too long, she thought with a private smile: best to find Costa quickly.

As she glided along the floor, sweeping her gaze over the gambling tables, she noticed eyes discreetly watching her. Her serene expression didn't falter, but her heartbeat increased as she scanned for any signs of trouble. She knew she looked elegant, but so did every other woman in here. If anything, Akke was barely keeping up, relying on her fine elven features to give her an advantage.

This thought lingered as she surveyed the room again, suddenly with new purpose.

"You're the only elf in here," Ailuros rumbled in her ear.

"You're right," she concurred, thinking quickly. She reached out to touch the arm of a passing pleasure boy.

He stopped immediately, turning a welcoming smile to her. "Does my lady require something?"

He was from the south, his dark skin and tightly coiled hair a stark contrast to a bold white tunic that left his muscular arms bare.

"I was meeting some friends here," she said with a little grin, "but I fear they may have started the party already. Have you seen them?" She brushed her fingers over her pointed ear. "They look like me."

"I wish we had more guests who look like you, my lady," the young man said, his voice deep and alluring. "But I haven't seen any of the fair folk here in ... months."

Before Akke could respond, he inched closer. "Perhaps I could entertain you until they arrive?"

She took a single step back. "Another time, perhaps. I think I see an acquaintance of mine just over there."

He bowed his head and, after one last look, retreated.

"No elves here in months?" Ailuros muttered. "Don't tell me the fey avoid gambling dens."

"Not usually," she replied, scanning the sea of human faces still surreptitiously watching her. "But apparently they avoid the Palace."

"You might have thought of that before we came in here."

"When I lived in Newport before, I wasn't exactly on the guest list to this sort of thing. How was I supposed to know?"

"Your vaunted Network?"

"Shut up," she hissed, "and let me think."

She took up her leisurely stroll again, keeping a pleasant smile pasted on her lips as she examined the room. The gambling tables filled most of the space, and on the far wall she could see two sets of wide stairways leading to a mezzanine level. Folk mingled on that second level in various states of inebriation and passion, and she could just make out a series of wooden doors leading further into the building for more discreet encounters. Was Costa planning to meet her in private? That would make sense, especially if he wanted to keep a low profile.

As she reached the centre of the gaming hall, she noticed a low, stone fountain. Water trickled steadily from it, pouring through well-worn channels to drop amongst half-dissolved statues depicting humans in all manner of debauchery and excess. Dozens of coins lay in the bottom of the pool that circled the fountain. The ring edging the pool was made of pure gold and carved into that gold were runes. Runes sharp and clearly carved in the Abyssal script.

"What is this?" Ailuros whispered, staring at the runes.

"I'd heard rumours," she breathed, "but I wasn't sure they were true. This place is more than a gambling hall and a brothel—it's a temple."

"To whom?"

"To Asmodeus, demon god of lust and obsession." She traced her fingers along one set of runes. "And to Mamnon, demon god of gluttony and excess."

"Didn't we just finish dealing with a demon god?"

"That was Eurynomos ... different one."

"But isn't this just as bad?"

"No." She hesitated. The demon gods were generally evil, but not all were totally shunned by civilization. She'd been taught that life was not without sin or suffering, and thus some worship of the demon gods—a select few of them—was tolerated. For instance, she knew that ordinary folk at times gave offerings or prayers to Akuma to ward away any misfortune.

But to flaunt their power so brazenly? It spoke volumes of the corruption in Newport that such a temple could exist.

"No," she said again, already turning her mind back to the task at hand. "It's not as bad. Neither of these two want to destroy the world."

"But this whole place is a shrine to them. Is that why your fey cousins stay clear?"

"Perhaps."

Akke spotted the black-haired escort slinking towards them again, hunger in her eyes. The whole business made Akke uneasy, especially when she thought about to whom this temple was dedicated. But this wasn't the time to overturn the Newport applecart. She was on a mission to save Ruthia and to do that, she realized, she had to play the game. And in a place like this, there was only one class of people who knew all the secrets.

She touched the arm of the girl as she moved into reach. Her pale skin very much on display in her form-fitting, scarlet dress cut up to her hips and down to her navel.

The woman wrapped her hand around Akke's, slipping her other around Akke's waist and pulling them together. "Let me serve you, milady," the woman said huskily. She stared at Akke with her dark blue eyes for a long moment, then glanced briefly at Ailuros with a seductive smile. "Your panthor can stand guard over us ... and watch."

Ailuros snorted, showing extreme disinterest in the suggestion.

"I have a better idea," Akke said, raising a coy eyebrow. "My friend is gambling, but I'd like to talk him into something else. Maybe you can help me."

"Of course."

"What's your name, darling?"

"Sarsha, milady."

"Perhaps you can help me find my friend, Sarsha." Akke made a show of looking around. "He's given me the slip, but he's here."

"I'm sure I know him. Tell me his name, milady."

"Costa, the famous explorer and merchant."

Sarsha's eyes lit up with either greed or lust. Or both.

"I can convince him to have you join us," Akke continued. "If you can take me to him."

The young lady slipped her arm around Akke's waist and directed her forward. Akke draped her arm over Sarsha's shoulders and played along.

"He's playing Dragons and Goblins in the inner sanctum," she said, leading them toward a wide stone arch that led deeper into the temple. She gave Akke a sidelong glance. "I assume milady is welcome in there?"

"Is there anywhere in this city an elf *can't go*?" she replied with touch of haughtiness.

Sarsha tensed slightly against her but continued to walk forward. "Of course not, milady."

The inner sanctum was guarded by a burly enforcer on each side of the archway. They watched Akke carefully as she approached, but Sarsha gave them a wave and they did nothing to stop the two women and their panthor escort from walking through.

Once through the arch, the heat rose noticeably. Sarsha slid her hand up Akke's back to deftly remove the fur stole from her shoulders. With a precision worthy of an escape artist, she handed the stole to an assistant who appeared from an alcove. He exchanged it for a small wooden card that she in turn handed to Ailuros.

Akke pointedly ignored the activity and surveyed the dim room. The ceiling was surprisingly high, with magic lanterns floating at regular intervals to bathe each table with a warm light. Gamblers sat around the wide tables in luxurious chairs as servants glided past with refreshments. The general noise of muted conversations was a faint rumble throughout the room. No one looked up from their game. For all the relaxed poses, Akke could tell that these games were for high stakes.

"There he is," Sarsha whispered in Akke's ear, jutting her chin to their right. "You can't miss that golden shirt."

Akke examined the nearby tables of card players. Sure enough, a broad-shouldered man in a flamboyant gold shirt was seated on the far side of a game. His brown hair hung straight past his shoulders, and his chiselled features were intent on the five cards held close to his chest. This was clearly a merchant who hadn't grown soft on his wealth. She'd never met Costa before, but she'd heard many stories, and if even half of them were true ... Well, she had her work cut out for her.

"Wait here," she said, patting the girl's hip.

She started forward but got barely five steps before an older gentleman in an impeccable black suit moved into view. "May I help you, my lady?"

His manner immediately revealed him as a guard, albeit the kind sent to shoo away unwanted fops and floozies. Akke could see at least two actual bodyguards with truncheons lurking in the shadows at the edge of the room.

She slowed, reaching up to press a delicate hand against the gentleman's lapel. "I'm here to meet my friend Costa. I can see him right there."

The gentleman sidestepped to discreetly block her progress. "I don't recall Master Costa mentioning that he was expecting a lady of the fair folk today."

"And are you his personal valet?" she asked sharply, leaning into her posh elven accent.

He started at her sudden tone.

"Is he expected to tell you everything?" she pressed. "Make him aware that I've arrived. Now."

He offered a curt smile and nodded. "Just a moment, my lady."

Akke stood her ground as the guard moved efficiently around the table, keeping a wide berth until he reached Costa. Leaning in, he whispered to the merchant. Costa looked up casually, sharp eyes coming to rest on Akke.

She lifted one hand almost lazily, running her fingers along the side of her neck. It was the pre-arranged greeting. Costa smiled, blowing her a kiss from his fingers, and beckoning her to join him.

Akke slinked forward. She was about to cast a triumphant glance at the gentleman guard, but the guard met her quickly and gestured to Ailuros in her wake. "Your bodyguard will have to wait here, my lady," he said firmly.

Not wanting to push their luck, Akke sighed heavily and turned to the panthor. "Keep Sarsha company," she said, looking over to where the escort watched intently. "Don't let her get talking to anyone else."

"You aren't actually planning on ...?"

"No! But she knows a lot—we need to keep her close, for now."

"As milady commands." Ailuros said with a slight mocking bow.

Ailuros retreated toward the entrance as Akke rounded the table of players, meeting Costa's eyes. He shuffled his chair to the side and a servant placed a padded stool into the open space, along with a fresh drink.

Akke slid into the seat and ran her hand affectionately up Costa's arm. A well-muscled arm, she noted immediately, to match the shoulders that her arm draped across. "Hello, my dear," she said, loudly enough for the other players to hear.

Costa gave her a sidelong smile, but then turned back to his cards. Akke knew the game well enough, and this round had moved into the critical bluffing stage. Costa kept his cards so close to his chest that even she couldn't see them, but her eyes were drawn to his actual chest where a loose, open collar revealed broad muscles. His posture was relaxed, but she could feel the energy coiled in his frame and knew that he was anything but ignorant of his surroundings.

As she settled into position her knee brushed against the curved, jewel-encrusted scabbard fastened to his broad belt. The hilt was ivory-infused steel, and she knew at a glance that the worn smoothness of it came from frequent use.

"It's called a *kilij*," he said to her, glancing down at the curved sword.

 An unusual weapon, one she knew was common in the various desert kingdoms to the south. "It's very impressive," she purred.

He turned back to his cards, made his bet, then upped it as the offer came round to him again.

"You can't be that lucky," a man across the table finally declared. "I call, Costa."

With a stony expression, Costa laid down his cards face up. A run of knights.

The man across the table threw down his cards in disgust.

"You'll have your time," Costa boomed with a chuckle. "Another hand?"

The man rose from the table and stormed off. The other patrons exchanged a few dry remarks, but Akke could tell there was a bad energy around the game. The dealer sensed it, too, and called for a short refreshment break. Most of the player rose, moving off into the room.

Costa pulled in his fresh winnings and motioned for one of his attendants to gather them up. He then turned in his chair, sizing up Akke fully for the first time. He was probably fifteen years her senior, and this close she could see creases by his eyes. But his smile was playful, and he moved with the easy confidence of a man in control of his world.

"So," he rumbled, "the god-slayer herself. I'm

honoured."

"Am I what you expected?" she asked with a sly grin.

His eyes inspected her, but in a manner different from the courtesans and patrons of the temple, appreciating her with a respect she found very refreshing. "You have strength in you, clearly, and if the stories are true, no shortage of courage." He glanced around the dim room filled with Newport's most powerful. "And you know your way around fine folk."

"This is child's play, my dear."

"It might seem so, to a daring adventurer fresh out of the wilderness," he countered with a raised eyebrow, "but rest assured there are dangers lurking everywhere. Some of them harder to see than others."

"Without doubt," she conceded. "I know that you've won many a battle both inside and outside Newport's walls."

"I try not to think of them as battles," he said. "More as … opportunities."

"The measure of a person is in how they use the opportunities they're given." She kept her voice a low purr, focusing on Costa as if he were her entire world.

"Or in how they make their own opportunities," he added with a simple nod of his head.

"Quite." Akke took a slow sip of her drink.

"Such as when you defeated the forces of two demon gods, and earned the favour of one of the most enigmatic champions of our age?" His expression was mild, but his eyes couldn't hide their interest.

He was subtle, and showed genuine interest in her, but his reference to Lord Persus gave her momentary pause. All too many powers had been making personal enquiries of the Champion of Light. The paladin of Helios was everything one could imagine, and more. But most of all, Persus had earned her friendship and trust. She wouldn't drag his name into any idle gossip.

So, she tried a diversion. "The threat was too great to ignore. It had been building for years: missing adventurers in the north, hobgoblin hordes in the south, the dead rising from their crypts..." She gave him a small smile. "And undead attacks on caravans bound for Newport."

The last was more than enough to get his full attention. Surprise flickered across his features. "You've heard stories."

"From what I understand, about six years ago one of your caravans was waylaid by an attack most foul, causing a flurry of wizards and priests to descend upon Newport's necropolis. That was just the start."

He was impressed, she could tell, but he allowed little more than a curious smile to shape his features. "And you were the end."

She carefully replaced her drink, crossing one knee over the other as she leaned into him. Her fingers traced along the back of his neck. "A girl does what a girl must."

He studied her for a long moment, then nodded toward the stone arch. "Is that why you brought Sarsha with you?" he asked. "To do as a girl must?"

Her smile didn't falter, but her stomach tightened as she realized that he was no fool. How had he even seen that while staying intent on his cards? She needed to be better; Ruthia's freedom depended on it.

"She just helped me find you. You can have her all to yourself later."

"Once she's finished reporting to her patron," he growled, eyes flicking again beyond Akke.

She turned her head slowly, quickly spotting the white fur of Ailuros and, several paces away, the scarlet dress of Sarsha as she spoke quickly to a tall, elderly man in robes.

The man looked right at Akke. Even from this distance she saw the recognition in his eyes. He knew her. Nobody other than street urchins and petty thugs in Newport knew her, except ...

"Oh, damn."

"Now," Costa mused, "what would the wizard in the long-time employ of Master Pellio want with you?"

Akke turned back. Her arm was still draped over Costa's shoulders and their faces were bare inches apart. He was still eyeing her with genuine curiosity, but there was a new intensity to his gaze. She wasn't hanging off him for fun; his cooperation was vital to her mission. What had been a leisurely dance was suddenly a sprint.

"I may have to leave soon," she said quickly, "so listen up. I'm trying to find an old friend, a street kid named Ruthia, to rescue her from this city. She's a servant girl with the Serpents, who work for the Guild. I need you to get me an introduction to the Guild so I can get her out."

His expression didn't shift. "So, what does Pellio want with you?"

She couldn't quite keep the smirk off her face. "I broke into his personal chambers a few years back. Nearly made it out, too."

"That was you?" New respect flashed in Costa's eyes. He let out a low laugh. "You sound like trouble."

She smiled anew, but he pulled back, slipping out from under her arm. "A little too much trouble. I appreciate you trying to find your friend, but I'm not picking a fight with Pellio just to do the Network a favour."

"Pellio's not important," she insisted. "I need you to talk to the Guild."

"It seems," he said, suddenly rising to his feet, hand on the hilt of his *kilij*, "that Pellio is of immediate importance, at least to you. Good day, my lady."

He stepped away, eyes beyond her, and Akke heard the rapid approach of footsteps.

She leapt to her feet, stool toppling backward, and spun around. A burly man in a leather jerkin was striding toward her, drawing his sword. Amidst sudden shouts of protest, he pushed aside the gentleman guard, eyes locking on Akke.

She thrust out her hand.

Sleep.

But just as her magic was released, something cut her spell like a knife. There was no other way to explain it. The approaching man jostled more patrons to the side, raising his sword as he closed. Akke desperately tried to cast another spell. No effect.

Her eyes darted around the room, just detecting the faint glow of magical glyphs on a nearby wall, no doubt the source of the *counterspells*. She cursed herself for a fool. The temple was warded, likely to prevent magical manipulation in games of chance. No wonder Pellio's wizard was still just standing there in the background. To make matters worse, Ailuros was grappling with two other brutes, too far away to help her.

The attacking man was upon her, swinging down with his sword. The blow was powerful enough to cleave her in two, but she nimbly stepped forward and under the blow. She grasped the descending forearm of his sword hand, extending her right hand under his other arm. Just like Osho had taught her, she pivoted, thrusting her hip against his. The hip toss sent the big man off his feet, his momentum carrying him forward. He flew over her shoulder and crashed heavily into the gambling table. As soon as he lifted his head, Akke's fist impacted his face.

Fire exploded through her knuckles as they crunched against solid bone. She winced and withdrew her hand—his head was like a cinderblock. He stared up at her unperturbed, then rose to his feet. He was a towering lunk of a man, but he smiled like a wolf as he stared down at her.

Without magic or daggers, Akke suddenly felt very small. Cursing herself for not somehow building weapons into her ensemble, she backed up and raised her hands, waiting to deflect his next blow.

Cinderblock stepped forward and raised his own meaty fists, ignoring his sword lying on the floor. He swung heavily, but Akke leant back, barely avoiding the blow. Then his fist returned in a surprising backhand swing. She rolled with the blow, but there was still enough force to knock her to the floor.

Staying low, she swept a powerful kick into his knee. It was like kicking a tree trunk. She rolled back as his giant boot slammed down toward her. Cinderblock reared up again, staring at her with new intensity. Looking around, he spotted his sword.

From Akke's left, a flash of green and white flew into view. Ailuros slammed into Cinderblock, toppling the man with a crash. The panthor's front paws closed around Cinderblock's throat while his back paws raked at the man's leather armour. The leather shredded under the onslaught, but Cinderblock ignored that attack to fight against the vice against his throat. With sheer strength, he removed the panthor's grasp. Ailuros, using all his feline grace, managed to stay on top as the brute bucked like a wild bull.

All around them, people were screaming and running, the temple's guards struggling to close in on the fight against the tidal surge of fleeing patrons. Even so, Akke knew they only had seconds to escape. The stone arch leading back to the main gambling hall was full of people, but Akke spotted Costa's golden shirt slipping out through what looked like a servant's door on the far wall. As Cinderblock finally succumbed to Ailuros' furious attack, she grabbed the panthor and hauled him into a run.

Shouts behind them indicated new pursuit, but neither slowed as they ran to the unguarded door. Akke was through in a flash, leaping over a wooden cart filled with dirty dishes. They were in the kitchens, she realized, and servants scrambled to get clear as she skidded her way around the chopping tables. Spying an ajar door, she sprinted for it and the moonlight it revealed, hearing the scrabble of claws behind her as Ailuros easily kept pace.

She burst through the door, her elven eyes adjusting quickly to the darkness. They were on the street, a large carriage with four horses occupying most of the space. She slowed but couldn't stop herself from sliding into the wooden side. Ailuros reached over her to grab the door and haul it open, pushing her up into the dark interior.

"Drive!" he roared.

Inside the cabin, Akke fell against something warm

and solid. She barely had time to look up beyond the golden fabric before Ailuros was pushing in behind her, slamming the door.

"Yes, Diana," boomed a deep voice, tapping the ceiling, "please do drive."

Looking up, she realized that she was more or less in the lap of Costa. Strong hands gripped her shoulders and gently helped her into the seat across from him. Ailuros flopped down next to her, peeking out through the curtains as the carriage lurched into motion.

Costa examined them both, a curious smile lighting his features.

"A half-elf bard and a white panthor in my carriage. Shall I also expect a half-orc warrior and a monk of Thanatos for dinner?"

Akke took a deep breath, assessing no malice in the man. "Zom is back on the frontier, and Osho is with his master. It's just us."

"I am sorry, my dear. I didn't know the monk fell." The apology was sincere.

She nodded, hanging on as the carriage wheeled around a sharp bend.

"But the stories *are* true." Costa turned his gaze to Ailuros. "Well met, noble panthor. You're handy in a scrap: those bodyguards of Pellio's you dispatched are no slouches, and the one assailing your mistress—well, he's as dumb as an iron post, but just as difficult to take down."

Ailuros dusted off his tunic and straightened his hat. "Speed and skill will overcome slow strength every time."

"Indeed." He paused in thought for a moment, then turned back to Akke. "Why are you trying to rescue this young friend of yours? Is she someone important?"

Something about Costa made her relax. He was an opportunist, for sure, but nothing in his demeanour suggested malice. He was also extremely well-connected, so creating false stories was probably unwise.

"No, she's no one important. A street urchin—one I failed to protect." Guilt twisted in her stomach, and she swallowed down the still-unfamiliar sensation. "Which is why I must rescue her from Newport. She has nobody, and I should have taken care of her years ago. I'm trying to fix that now."

The coach slowed and turned again. Through the curtains, Akke could see that they'd entered a small courtyard. With a clatter of hooves, the horses stopped. A creak from above indicated that the driver was descending.

The door opened and a woman looked up into the cabin. She was likely ten years Akke's senior, fit and striking.

"Are we entertaining guests?" she asked mildly.

"Thank you, Diana," Costa replied, "for your driving skills. I assume we weren't followed?"

Her withering glare was answer enough, and he offered her an amused smile. He gestured at Akke and Ailuros. "Diana, may I introduce my new friends—members of the Fierce Force itself. And from what I saw back at the Palace, the stories are true."

Diana sized them up quickly, as if meeting heroic figures from the frontier was an everyday occurrence. From what Akke knew of Costa's Curios, it might be. "What brings you to Newport?" she asked.

"I'm looking for a friend," Akke replied.

"Does anyone else know this?" Costa interjected.

"That your friend is your goal?"

Akke waved this off. "Just a couple of petty crime bosses who were able to tell me that she's with the Serpents."

"Do those petty crime bosses know who you are?" he asked.

"I knew them when I was a street urchin myself."

Costa nodded, thinking. His eyes moved between Akke and Ailuros.

"Why?" Akke pressed, worry joining the guilt in her gut.

"I suspect at least one of them told Pellio you were back in town. Did Sarsha come and find you?"

Akke thought back. Sarsha was one of several pleasure companions to make advances on her.

"Because," Costa continued, "word was already spreading through the Palace that a half-elf and a panthor were in the building. I saw Pellio react, and he immediately directed his minions to find you. I guess Sarsha was first— she's always been an excellent predator."

Diana's sharp laugh was dripped in acid.

"So," Akke said slowly, "Pellio knows I'm here." She felt herself go cold. This development wasn't unexpected, but she'd hoped desperately to avoid it.

"That complicates things," Costa concluded.

"Why?"

"I'd like to help you," he said, shrugging broadly. "You have a noble spirit, and you're here on a worthy cause. But my business relies on my good relations with all power-brokers in this city. If I'm known to have helped you despite

Pellio's wrath, it will cost me."

"I'm sure I can muster the appropriate gold," she muttered. She wasn't sure at all, and her mind skipped from Patrick to Regwald, and even to Lord Persus back in Sanctuary, for people she could hit up for a loan.

Costa and Diana exchanged a glance.

"My dear," Costa said with a frown, "you need to learn a few things more about how Newport works. Gold makes the machine run, but our real currency is favours."

This was getting frustrating. Akke took another deep breath, calming herself. "So, if you introduce me to the Guild, what do you require in exchange?"

"Is Dannyk still injured?" Costa suddenly asked Diana.

"Yes," she replied, "and after his latest defeat he wasted the rest of his money on drinks and whores. He's got nothing left for healing potions, even at our rates."

Costa smiled as he looked at Ailuros. "What I need ... is a fighter."

The panthor grinned as an anticipatory snarl escaped his lips. "Show me the prey."

"I don't need a killer," Costa clarified. "I need a fighter. Someone who can turn a fight into a dance, who can dazzle the crowd, who can *entertain*."

"You need a gladiator?"

"Of sorts. No weapons, just strength, speed, and skill. Not to the death, but it's still a dangerous game. Your claws will be taped, but otherwise all your natural abilities are yours to do with as you please. One match—tomorrow afternoon."

"Just one match?" Ailuros' tail swished in obvious

interest.

"Against a former contender, trying to hold onto the glory of his youth and make one more run at the city title. Give him the fight of his life." Costa turned to Akke. "And you, my dear, have my word. You *will* receive your introduction."

"I'm in." Ailuros growled before she could consider her response.

CHAPTER 5

Akke followed Costa and Diana into the arena, keeping her wide cap low over her features even as her eyes were drawn upward to the spectacle around her. She'd seen the massive façade of Newport's giant temple to Aris—god of strategy, honour, and war—many times in her youth, but she'd never set foot inside the Rings of Glory before. And despite her many years travelling the realms, she'd never seen anything like this.

Ten thousand citizens crowded in on rising rows of seats that created a vast circle around the central fighting pit. The stone frame of the arena rose higher than most city walls and great, retracted awnings billowed colourfully in the evening breeze. The roar of the people was so deep she felt it in her bones, like an army just before the advance. But these were no warriors gathered around her: they were regular folks from Newport and its many surrounding villages. From children to the elderly, from working class to the elite, all gathered in anticipation of battle and glory.

The cold was absent and, despite the roof open to the late winter's chill, Akke sweltered under her bulky jerkin and trousers. Her plain outfit was purposefully too big, its bulk hiding her feminine figure just as her wide cap covered her pointed ears and masked her fine features. She'd even glued horsehair to her chin as a shaggy goatee to complete her disguise as a young man—just another hopeful novice following in the wake of the great Costa.

The early bouts had already happened, and the arena was at capacity as the afternoon's main event approached. Akke was just one of many people moving to and from seats as the temple acolytes efficiently tore down the wooden towers used in the last group fight and set up an archery range. A quick marksmanship competition was next on the bill, apparently a fan favourite despite its lack of explicit violence.

Costa glanced back, directing Akke to a spot at the end of the bench in the second row. He then took his own seat just in front of her, greeting the other wealthy patrons nearby.

Diana sat next to Costa, looking all business in her leather armour and pair of short swords on her belt. A wealthy man and his obvious bodyguard, they drew many gazes from other members of the elite—and none of those gazes, Akke noted with satisfaction, included her: the invisible young man in the second row. The man next to Akke glanced at her once, offered a quick nod, and then turned back to his friends. Happy to disappear into the crowd, Akke slumped in on herself and observed.

The ringside row was unique for having seats rather than benches, and the general wardrobe of its occupants immediately revealed their wealth. There were no ostentatious displays of gold or jewellery, but only the finest fabrics of imported mulberry silks, fine linens and luxurious furs were on display, and the tailoring of each outfit was exquisite. Servants hovered during this intermission to offer food and drink, and many quiet conversations between the elite were clearly more than idle chatter about the entertainment. Akke didn't know their faces, but she could read the body language to determine who were the true holders of power and who were the supplicants.

Costa was clearly one of the former. He made no effort to rise from his seat, sitting comfortably with a drink as others came to him. Diana on the other hand, watched each supplicant closely, eyeing them as potential threats.

He was first greeted by one of the priests of Aris, who thanked him for sponsoring so many great fighters. Next came a city councillor, his purple sash of office worn proudly over his tunic. He took a few minutes to discuss the viability of establishing a new trade route to help avoid Middle Kingdom duties when travelling to the Southern Desert Kingdoms. Costa indicated his interest in pursuing it but stressed the many dangers lurking on the wilderness back roads. The councillor assured him that certain upcoming tax breaks for key merchants would help Costa free up the necessary funds to support an expedition.

A younger man stopped by, concern on his face. "Master Costa, I heard that Dannyk is hurt! Is there going to be fight tonight?"

"Dannyk was injured, yes, and he was unable to spare the expense for healing." Costa shook his head in a show of regret, and then smiled. "But there will still be a fight."

"Who would dare challenge the Bear?"

"Patience, son. Costa's Curios has a little surprise in store."

The young man grinned, nodded his thanks, and then retreated.

Akke tugged her wide hat lower when she spotted the tall, elderly wizard from the Palace. There were no magic wards that she could detect here, and the last thing she wished was to face another wizard in combat. He was on his feet, walking a pace behind another tall man. Akke recognized him immediately.

Pellio had hardly changed since their last meeting, except this time he was clothed and awake. Middle-aged and stern, the merchant prince towered over the seated Costa as he strode over, his long robes hanging straight off his slender form. An elegant broach held his outer cloak fastened across his chest, and a felt hat covered his balding head. Deep-set eyes looked down a long nose, and when he smiled his face crinkled.

"Good afternoon, Master Costa," he said.

"Master Pellio," Costa replied, rising from his chair in respect. And, Akke realized, effectively hiding her. "I don't often see you here at the games."

"I rarely have the time." He spared a quick glance of contempt at the crowds around them. "But I know it's one of your favourite forms of entertainment."

"I do enjoy a good demonstration of strength."

There was a pause, but Akke didn't dare look up to see what was going on.

Pellio's feet stepped closer to Costa. "That elf girl you were talking to yesterday at The Palace, who is she?"

"I don't really know. I didn't have time to find out before your thug attacked me."

"He was attacking her, actually—"

"I couldn't tell the difference."

Diana rose to her feet. There was nothing threatening in her movements, but the tension suddenly rose.

There was another pause. Akke could feel a bristle

of magic in the air; perhaps the wizard was projecting a protective spell around Pellio? A place like this was certainly a good spot for an assassin to hide.

"I apologize," Pellio said finally. "It was a mistake. And now I wonder if the girl herself was who I thought she was. I was hoping you could enlighten me."

"She was an adventurer from the wilds," Costa said smoothly, "looking to join my merchant house. I understand she's a bit of a mercenary, but that's all I got before we were rudely interrupted."

"Again, my apologies."

"And accepted with humility, Master Pellio. An honest misunderstanding, I'm sure. But clearly this elf is a threat. Perhaps one of my teams could escort your next caravan, to keep it safe from her and her comrades?"

Always making the opportunity, Akke thought with a tiny smile. Costa was good.

"I'm sure that would be fine." Pellio sniffed.

"Always a pleasure, Master Pellio."

"One more thing. If that girl does contact you again, please do let me know. I would consider it a great favour."

"Then I will keep my eyes peeled."

"Good day, Master Costa."

The magic field drifted away as Pellio and his wizard retreated. Costa sat down and took a leisurely sip of his drink, then settled back in his chair. Akke hunched forward.

"I just passed on earning a great favour, *boy*. Your cat better be worth it."

She didn't need to boast. "You saw him in action."

A hush fell over the crowd, signalling the beginning

of the archery tournament, which was apparently the final stage of a weeks-long event.

A man in a dazzling white suit and hat took centre-stage, his voice easily able to reach every corner of the arena thanks to the amazing acoustics of the temple.

"Ladies and gentlemen," he boomed, "please welcome back to the Rings of Glory our three archery finalists!"

Akke listened idly as their names were heralded, each to wild applause, and watched as two men and an elven woman emerged along the wide path leading from the bowels of the temple. Excitement rippled through the crowd, and she had to admire the temple's ability to fire up emotions.

As the tournament got underway, Akke watched the shots with growing respect, though she still kept most of her attention on the crowd. Pellio and his wizard seemed engrossed in the entertainment, but she doubted they were alone.

When a huge roar from the crowd erupted around her, Akke realized that the tournament was over. The young elven woman hefted her bow in triumph, accepting the handshakes of her two fellow finalists. No surprise really; elves were the finest archers in all the lands.

As the archers exited down the contestants' wide corridor, another flurry of acolytes saw the targets removed and a series of welded iron bars drawn in by cart. As servants passed by with a final round of refreshments, the acolytes constructed an iron cage big enough to hold thirty men. Four walls of bars rose up to an open top with a single, hinged door on one side.

The announcer stepped through that door, followed

by a hulking cleric in full plate armour bearing the blazing spear emblem of Aris. Akke was instantly reminded of another cleric of Aris that she knew: Gorak, one of the leaders of Sanctuary. It was clear this warrior would be the official in charge of the upcoming bout.

Standing inside the cage, the announcer raised his hands and a new hush fell over the arena. "Ladies and gentlemen. The Rings of Glory is proud to give you: the main event!" A roar of anticipation interrupted him. He let it sweep over him, then motioned again for quiet. "Introducing our first combatant!"

Deep, rhythmic drums pulsed through the arena as all eyes went to the man-sized cage being pushed out on a cart by six acolytes.

"Deep from the dark jungles of the south, where men fear to tread, the courageous explorers of Costa's Curios captured this mighty beast."

Akke stared at the cage where a white, furred shape prowled on four legs, hissing and roaring at the crowd as only a cat could. The rumble of anticipation began to grow as the cart reached the main cage, and the acolytes pushed the smaller cage against the door. Ailuros swiped upward at the pair of acolytes who scrambled onto his cage and together lifted one side to open access to the fighting stage.

"Ladies and gentlemen, guard yourselves against ... the mighty Cat-Man of the jungles of Sizweeee!"

Ailuros leapt from his cage, landing on two feet and turning to roar at the crowd. The sheer sound was terrifying, and gasps erupted all around her. Akke looked at her friend with new respect. Now staying upright, he was dressed in barely a loincloth, his white fur bristling as he flexed his muscles and turned to roar at another section of the crowd. The crowd thundered in response.

"And his opponent!"

Trumpets sounded in the distance, the kind that might herald the arrival of a king. From the end of the contestants' corridor a man appeared, lumbering forward with determination. The crowd started to cheer even as the announcer boomed over them.

"From the humble docks of Newport he came, making his name as a mighty, unstoppable warrior. Twice robbed of a championship laurel, he has now returned, stronger than ever, and ready to earn his right to challenge. Welcome back to the Rings of Glory ... Jedrik, the Beeeeeaaar, Vettonos!"

Akke was stunned at the tidal wave of noise that washed over her. She found herself on her feet, driven by the excitement of the crowd as they cheered their long-time favourite. She remembered hearing tales of Jedrik in her youth: a formidable fighter who always seemed to get unlucky right when he had the chance to become the champion. He'd been an idol for the boys around her, and clearly was still a fan favourite despite his advancing years.

The Bear bounded up onto the stage, stepping through the cage door and flexing for the crowd. A beast of a man, his muscles rippled under thick, black body hair. His shaved head gleamed in the lanterns floating overhead, and his walrus moustache danced as he shouted back at the crowd. The adulation continued for a few moments.

Part of her wanted to laugh at the sheer spectacle, but her eyes instinctively went to Pellio. The man was frozen in his seat, staring at Ailuros. Then he glanced around and whispered to a man sitting next to him. That man rose, gripping his scabbard as he jogged out of the arena.

Akke slunk lower in her chair. There were only so many white panthors in this world, and doubtless only one in all of Newport. And that white panthor was a known associate of hers. Pellio knew she was here.

A clanging bell announced the start of the match. The announcer scrambled through the gate and slammed it shut behind him, leaving the cleric and combatants behind.

Ailuros and the Bear circled each other, both grinning in anticipation. A few testing strikes by both men were exchanged as they tried to get the measure of the other. Then the Bear charged.

Ailuros moved to dodge but was surprised by the speed with which Jedrik closed the distance. The Bear managed to get one arm under Ailuros' armpit, while pinning the panthor's other arm to his side in a classic wrestling move. He swept his leg, completing the move and tripping the cat-man.

Ailuros fell, but before Jedrik could pin him the panthor scrambled free, leaping clear of danger. The crowd gasped.

Jedrik charged forward again, but Ailuros was already in motion, evading the follow-up attempts to grapple and lashing out with stiff jabs, followed by kicks to the Bear's legs. Akke recognized Ailuros' fighting style: a hit-and-run tactic used many times by Osho against larger opponents.

Ailuros danced around the cage, baiting the Bear and scoring some hits while dodging most of those sent in return. The two fighters exchanged blocks and feints with impressive ability. Jedrik knew how to fight with his hands, but Ailuros was clearly faster. The crowd loved it, permanently on their feet as they cheered. Akke stood as well. It made it easier to blend in, and easier to keep an eye out for any of Pellio's men.

In the cage, Jedrik staggered back as Ailuros caught him with a heavy strike. But his momentary stumble was a feint and, as the panthor tried to seize the moment, Jedrik reversed his momentum. He ducked under the panthor's punches, ramming his shoulder into the midsection of the cat-man and driving him off his feet.

Ailuros toppled, pinned, as the big man landed on top and rained down blows from a mounted position. Ailuros desperately tried to block the hammer fists, but the beating was savage.

The bell clanged to end the round, the all-but-forgotten official stepping in to immediately separate the combatants.

Jedrik released Ailuros and stood, basking in the adulation of the crowd. He strode back to his corner and sipped some water. Ailuros picked himself up slowly and moved to his own corner, clearly angry with his performance thus far.

Around the arena, Akke saw movement. A few fans came and went during the break between rounds, but most were planted in their seats, raving about the fight so far. The movement she tracked was different—focused and coordinated.

Men walked the aisles between the benches, scanning left and right carefully. They were looking for her; she knew it.

Akke tugged her hat down further to ensure her ears were covered. As she watched, one man stopped and questioned a citizen—an elf, by the look of her clothing—in an exchange that nearly became violent through his aggression, and the indignation of the elf woman's bodyguard. Other goons noticed the disturbance and closed in. One of them arrived to take a good look at the elf, then shook his head, apologising profusely for the misunderstanding and defusing the situation.

Akke knew that to leave her seat would only draw attention. She had to trust in her disguise and her anonymity in the crowd. As the bell rang to commence the second round, she rose again to her feet and cheered, looking for all the world like a typical fan.

Ailuros was looking good despite the beating he'd received in the first round, and he used his superior speed to strike with jabs, repeatedly evading Jedrik's counter-strikes to crack away at Jedrik's right leg. The Bear kept trying to grapple, but the panthor's persistence paid off as he made strike after careful strike while slowing the big man down.

Once more Jedrik managed to pull Ailuros in for a 'bear hug,' but before he could secure another takedown, the panthor kicked off the ground and threw his legs backwards, pushing off the bars. The crowd roared as the panthor, his feline agility on full display, somersaulted over the Bear.

Jedrik turned, obviously limping now, and took a kick to the face. He staggered, raising his arms to block Ailuros' next strike, but the panthor pounced again. A flying knee—a favourite move of Osho's—cracked into Jedrik's skull, sending him tumbling backwards into the side of the cage.

Ailuros threw himself in another attack as the crowd screamed in appreciation, and his full weight crashed into the Bear. The human crumpled to the ground in a daze. The bell clanged, but Ailuros didn't let up his attack. The cleric of Aris had to pull Ailuros back with both armoured hands.

Ailuros shook himself free and rallied the crowd, roaring to the sky. The crowd roared back in approval. Despite the first-round beating, he was winning both this fight and the crowd.

Jedrik staggered to his corner and reached for a ladle of water. But while the official was scolding Ailuros to follow his instructions and the sound of the bell at the end of a round, Jedrik pulled a small wooden flask from his loincloth. In a smooth motion, he uncorked and downed the entire thing. Akke watched closely as the welts under Jedrik's eyes receded. When he stood up, he did so with new vigour, no limp to his leg, and a new spring in his step.

Costa leant back in his seat and smiled in satisfaction. "Your panthor is truly remarkable," he mused without glancing at her. "And profitable."

That healing potion Jedrik had just downed, Akke suddenly realized, had likely been supplied by none other than Costa himself. Healing potions were very expensive, and tonight would no doubt be profitable for the merchant.

In the cage, Ailuros roared, riling up the crowd again as the bell signalled the start of the third round. But Akke's eyes were drawn away from the action to movement on the floor in front of her: Pellio's goons had reached the lower rows in their search. From the crashes against the cage and the cheers of the crowd, she knew the fighters were putting on a good show—she just hoped it was enough to distract the searching goons.

She chanced a look at the cage where Ailuros was still dancing away from the Bear's heavy blows. But it was clear the panthor was tiring: his own strikes were far less accurate, and he blocked more than dodged. His body was like liquid as he escaped another grapple attempt, but as he leapt to safety up the cage wall, Jedrik's huge hand closed around his hind leg. With awesome power, the big human wrenched the panthor off the bars, throwing him down on the ground. To a thunderstorm of fan support, he held onto Ailuros' leg and used his whole body to swing him around again, smashing into the cage.

"Hey," came a sudden, gruff, voice. "Let me see your face."

Akke cursed herself for getting too involved with the fight. A man loomed beside her, pressing right into her space.

"Back off," she retorted in as deep a voice as she could muster. "I'm watching the fight!"

"Hey, Blade," the man called, grabbing Akke's arm, "come check out this one."

Blade. That little bastard. No surprise that he sold her out to Pellio. And there was no doubt he could identify her, even through her disguise. Below her hat's brim she saw Blade jog over from another aisle, mere moments away.

Akke summoned her magic, aiming it up an aisle behind Blade. Her whispered incantation was mostly drowned out by the roar of the crowd, and thankfully mistaken as a muttering complaint by the thug holding on to her. She flicked her fingers at her side.

"Hey, Blade!" The illusory voice cried out. *"I see her—she's running!"*

Blade spun immediately, barely scanning the aisles behind him before shouting for all his men to follow. The goon released Akke's arm and ran in pursuit. They charged up the steps of the arena.

Diana glanced over her shoulder. "Nice move."

Beyond, Ailuros was staggering, having finally freed himself from the Bear's grip with a flurry of vicious elbows against the man's head. Jedrik stumbled back but gathered himself quickly and advanced again: right into a spinning back kick that caught him painfully in the midsection.

Ailuros was tiring, though, while Jedrik seemed fresh thanks to the potion running through his veins. Jedrik shook off the blow with a laugh, drawing a gasp from the crowd. Ailuros threw a few more follow-up strikes, then recoiled as Jedrik struck back.

Ailuros ducked under a left hook, countering with a beautiful rip to the man's ribs, but the Bear answered the blow with an uppercut. Ailuros tried to dodge out of the way, but Jedrik's ham fist just clipped the panthor's jaw. Even the glancing blow was enough to send the panthor crashing to the ground. Jedrik followed up to finish the contest.

The final round rang out and the cleric of Aris grappled Jedrik from behind to stop his forward motion.

The crowd was on its feet, cheering. A number of scuffles flared up as arguments broke out among spectators over who had won. Acolytes scrambled through the crowds, trying desperately to maintain order in the arena.

The cleric of Aris moved both combatants to the middle of the fighting pit, holding each man's arm on either side of him. He suddenly raised Jedrik's hand high in the air.

Ten thousand citizens roared as one, and Jedrik 'the Bear' Vettonos claimed another win in his sunset climb to glory. He paraded around the cage, drinking in the adulation as Ailuros opened the cage, pounding his paw against the metal in frustration before slinking out.

Costa turned to Akke, obviously pleased. "Let's go, before Pellio's goons come back." Keeping his bulk between her and the still-seated Pellio, Costa joined the first of the crowd moving to exit the arena.

"I assume we still have a deal?" Akke muttered.

"I'm a man of my word, *boy*."

*

The moon was already setting by the time Akke stepped out into the alley behind Costa's favourite tavern. It was still several hours before dawn, and the city was at its coldest and quietest. The perfect setting to meet a senior member of the Thieves' Guild.

It had taken two nights to make the necessary arrangements, but Costa had come through. The time spent waiting had provided ample opportunity for Ailuros to rest and, more importantly, heal his wounded pride.

There were worse fates, Akke thought, than spending a couple days lounging in a luxurious manor. And it had worked out well for them, as the Network reported Pellio's agents were prowling the streets in search of the duo.

She heard a single creak as Ailuros slinked his way across the roof of the building to her left, his low shape barely visible against the starry sky. He had his spear in hand, ready to assist if necessary. Behind her was the empty end of the alley, and ahead of her was the shadowy space between the tavern and the shuttered storefront next door. She scanned the low rooftops and saw no other movement. Taking a slow, silent breath, she waited.

"Your cat is good," a silken voice drifted out of the darkness with a laugh. "If this had been on his turf, I honestly might not have noticed him."

A figure stepped from the deepest shadows, tall and confident. He wore a form-fitting cloak that revealed nothing except his leather boots, and these moved soundlessly as he walked.

"But these streets talk to me," he continued, closing so that she could see his narrow features inside the hood. "Every creak of an awning, every gust of wind through a narrow alley, every misstep of an aspiring thief. I assure you, Akke of Sanctuary, you are quite safe here."

"I thank you for the assurances," she replied, ignoring her surprise that a Newport elf was part of the Guild. "And for your assistance."

"I have done nothing for you," he replied lazily, "other than not turn you over to Pellio."

"And I thank you for that. Perhaps we can help each other?"

"I understand you seek a girl?"

"Yes, a human named Ruthia, perhaps thirteen summers. She's under the protection of the Serpents."

"I know of the one you speak. She belongs to us."

"Willingly?" she blurted before she could stop herself.

"Does it matter?"

The cool disdain this elf exuded set her blood astir, but she maintained her calm. Threats were no use here.

"I would like to see her freed," she said simply.

"And I care not whether she goes or stays. But we never give up something for free."

Everything had a cost in Newport. But she was so close now—she couldn't falter. "What," she asked slowly, "is the going rate for a human girl of her age?"

The elf stood in silence for a long moment. When he spoke again, there was a dangerous edge to his voice. "She is not for sale, Akke."

Akke thought about what Costa had said about the true currency of the city. "Then you want a favour from me." She waited expectantly, but no further response came. She suppressed a sigh, realizing he wasn't going to demand— she had to offer. "What might I do for you?"

"There is a book that I would like to have. Nothing special, nothing magical, nothing . . ." She suddenly felt his keen gaze upon her, "like a certain tome I hear that you've held in your very hands ... just a book."

That didn't mean it still couldn't be trouble. "And where can I find this book?"

"In an office desk on the fourth floor of the manor house at the corner of Griffon Street and Lilac Lane."

The sheer banality of the answer hung in the darkness between them. He was enjoying this, she knew, which meant she had to be on her guard. She didn't know the particular address but could guess by the street names that it was in Light Town.

"You're a guild of thieves," she said with a coy smile. "Why would you need me?"

"Because every thief we've sent is found the next morning, dead on the floor of the office. No cuts, no bruises, no magic burns. Just death by suffocation. There must be some kind of magic at play, but no one knows what." He stepped forward. "You have experience with both magic and robbery—no doubt this will be a simple jape for you."

The Guild was powerful enough to hire magic users. What was he not telling her? "Who owns this manor?"

"A mid-level city official. No one of note."

"And this book ... I'm guessing it has information in it that could severely compromise someone who *is* of note."

A soft laugh chilled the air even further. "Very good, *charfirya*."

Akke bristled at the casual insult. *Charfirya* literally translated as 'half-human' in the Elvish tongue, but its true meaning meant 'betrayer' or 'traitor.'

"The city official and the book," he continued blandly, "are both owned by a certain merchant prince whom I believe you already know. At least, no one else ever came so close to robbing Master Pellio in one of his inner sanctums."

His casual insult was forgotten when she heard that name again. "You want me to steal from Pellio? He already wants me dead."

"Then you have nothing to lose. And the life of dear Ruthia to gain."

Pellio, it seemed, was obsessed with her. Breaking into one of his strongholds again was perhaps the worst idea she'd heard since her idiot friends had made a deal with a dragon.

"Surely," she said, forcing a smile to her face, "there is another way we can come to an arrangement."

"I already grow bored with this conversation. I care nothing about whether your little pet human lives or dies, but I *am* interested in that book. If you get it, you can have her."

"And if I'm caught?"

"Then your precious *Network* has made an enemy of Pellio, and the Guild continues on as always."

Patrick was not going to like this one bit.

"Let me think about it," she said.

He had already turned away. "I don't care," he said. "The book for the girl. Try to do it before she dies of old age."

He disappeared silently into the shadows.

Moments later, Ailuros landed softly beside her. "Well?" he asked.

She stared up at him, mind racing. "We need a plan."

Chapter 6

"You're insane," Patrick stated flatly, showing perhaps the most emotion Akke had ever seen in him.

"Thanks for your support," she replied, downing the last of her tea.

They sat in the dining room of his manor with Ailuros and Regwald. The sunlight streaming through the windows gave a false sense of warmth—the day outside was still frosty, and so was the mood around the table.

"You have our support," Patrick said, rubbing the bridge of his nose in exasperation. "But what you're asking, well . . . "

"Yeah," she said, feeling her frustration grow, "it's a risk. Almost like, I don't know ... sneaking into the lair of an ancient dragon. And then, just after that, stopping a thousand-year-old warlock priest from summoning a demon general into the world."

She could feel herself rising from her chair, but Patrick gestured for her to sit. "The Network recognizes your service, Akke. And as Arch-Mage Abarax made clear, you will never again be called upon to serve against your will."

"But I am still part of the Network, yes? I can still request its resources?"

"Did the Network not track down that fellow, Cutter?"

Regwald interjected. "And get you an invitation to the Palace?"

"And I hope your accommodations have been acceptable," Patrick added.

Akke unclenched the fists in her lap, forcing calm on herself. The last few days navigating the cesspool that was Newport had dredged up too many unpleasant memories, and she knew it was wearing at her patience.

"I'm grateful for everything," she said finally. She took a deep breath. "But Ruthia is so close. I can't stop now. Since the Network won't give me a crew of fighters to go in and free her from the Serpents, I have to do what the Thieves' Guild asks. Those are my only two options."

Her glare silenced any words from either of the men that might suggest just walking away. That was not an option.

"Ailuros and I have been observing the manor house for the past two days," she continued. "We have a good sense of the staff's movements and the pattern of the guards provided by the city. Having your men cause a distraction just after sunset is the best time. The city watch is at its most vulnerable and the guards will have no choice but to respond—even for just a few minutes."

Patrick sighed again. "What you're asking of Regwald's crew is ... risky."

"Not really. If they soak the warehouse wall in oil beforehand, without anyone seeing them, the actual lighting of the fire will only take moments."

"And what if they're seen?" Patrick countered. "What if they're identified?"

"I could lose my ability to trade in Newport," Regwald

added.

Akke bit her tongue against a retort she would regret. She didn't *care* about that right now. Even if it happened, Regwald would be fine. Ruthia would not. "No doubt a few coins would convince any witnesses to stay silent," she said instead. "I'm willing to provide them."

"And what if one of those witnesses is part of the city corruption?" Patrick retorted. "That's a *lot* of coins."

"Surely," Ailuros grumbled, "you have other ways of ensuring their compliance."

"The Network has influence, yes," Patrick said quietly, "but not without limits."

"And burning down a city-owned warehouse isn't the kind of trouble we can use our influence to avoid," Regwald reminded her.

The ship captain seemed as perturbed as Patrick. Newport was the largest trading port between the frontier and the Middle Kingdoms—losing his standing here was something he wouldn't risk without due consideration. But Regwald was a merchant, and Akke knew he was always looking for a profitable trade.

"If this works," she said, staring straight at Regwald, not allowing herself to hesitate and consider what she was about to commit to, "*I* will owe a favour. A big one." She held his eye contact, watching as he studied her for sincerity.

She heard Patrick sigh behind her. "This is an insane plan."

"Drawing the guards away from our target house is essential," she retorted, rounding on him. "It has to happen for Ailuros and me to have any chance of getting inside."

"Do you have anyone else who could do this?" Regwald

suddenly asked Patrick.

Unable to hide his surprise at the question, Patrick shook his head. "I'm not willing to risk local Network assets," he said. "Not because we don't have the ability, but because if anyone is caught—and that includes you, Akke— all of Newport will know that the Network moved openly against Pellio. I can't have that."

"My individual crew members can't be tied back to the Network," Regwald pointed out.

Patrick sat back in his chair, his gaze flicking from Regwald to Akke. "Risking the *Fortune's Caress*, her crew, and her captain is a huge risk," he said. "I hope you understand what's at stake here, Akke."

In other words, she realized without too much surprise, this support was going to cost her. The Network's favours were never cheap. And favours were always, eventually, repaid.

"I do," she said, meeting his gaze fearlessly.

"Then let's do this!" Ailuros exclaimed, slapping his paw in the table. "Let's burn the warehouse, break into the castle, snatch the treasure, and rescue the damsel!"

She couldn't stop her grin. Honestly, that idiot panthor would charge into the thirteenth layer of hell if she asked him.

Patrick and Regwald both rose.

"We'll make preparations," the ship captain said, "and be ready to go for just after sunset."

*

Griffon Street was bustling with well-to-do pedestrians, Light Town's magic lamps already glowing as the last, orange rays of sunset faded. Akke kept her fur-lined cloak wrapped tightly around her to hide her gear but kept her hood down to maintain full awareness of her surroundings. Although the magic lamps' warmth cast a soft glow over the street, she was confident that the prevailing dim illumination would prevent anyone from identifying her at a glance. An elf out for an evening stroll along the shops of Griffon Street would draw little attention.

A white panthor, however, was sure to set tongues wagging, especially in the wake of that epic cage match in the Rings of Glory only a few nights ago. So Ailuros walked beside her with his hood fully up and obscuring his features.

The crowd hid them in plain sight, and Akke made a show of examining the wares on display at every third or fourth storefront. Enough to make her movements natural, but not enough to draw any hopeful vendors into conversation.

One darker building broke the string of trade along the street: a city-owned warehouse that stood in shadowy contrast to the bustling shops around it. But even so the warehouse wasn't completely quiet. In front of it, three men unloaded small barrels of oil. One of them muttered as he tripped while carrying a barrel, the contents splashing down the wood of the warehouse front. In his quiet movements he managed to kick over a second barrel, and the contents spilled out along the ground.

Akke cast a single glance at a fourth man supervising the debacle. He glanced back at her, hefting his pipe and the unlit match in his hands.

She and Ailuros moved past without breaking stride.

The intersection with Lilac Lane was almost upon them, and Akke's eyes were drawn to the private residence looming across the street.

She often suspected that the truly rich and powerful were the hardest to spot—so confident in their status that they felt no need to flaunt it. But this manor house clearly belonged to someone of rising station who wanted still more. Obviously, a recent construction, the stone house filled every available scrap of land between the roads and the neighbouring buildings. There was no courtyard, no gardens, no distance between the cobbled roads and the sheer walls that rose up in imposing strength. Any windows at ground level were little more than arched slits, as if barbarian hordes were expected to storm the building any day.

The second storey continued the upward march of stone, interrupted occasionally by coloured glass windows that were laced with intricate lead framework. Only at the third storey did the stone walls finally end—in crenelations, naturally—with the suggestion of an open-area patio before the recessed walls rose further.

Finally, in the corner closest to the main road, a circular tower stretched upward another three or four man-heights. It was capped by a red, conical roof and a golden weathervane.

"It really is ugly," she muttered. "No taste whatsoever."

"All the more satisfying," Ailuros rumbled, "to crack it open."

Glancing both ways to ensure no carriages were clattering past, they crossed Griffon Street and sat down at one of the empty tables outside a lavish café. A serving girl hurried out to greet them, shivering as she gently invited them to take a seat inside.

"I find the air refreshing," Akke said haughtily, barely looking at her. "Bring us tea."

The girl retreated and Akke peered across the narrow span of Lilac Lane to the far corner of the manor. There, an archway was built into the stone wall just before it pressed up against the older house squeezed in behind it. As the servants' entrance, it was well-used throughout the day, but even more so after sunset when the day staff went home, and the dinner scraps were dealt with. The glow from the magic lamps lining Griffon Street didn't quite reach the archway, leaving the rear of the house in shadows.

"The city guards are following their routine," Ailuros said.

As expected, there were three men dressed in the broad tunic bearing Newport's coat of arms: a two-mastered merchant ship on a background of blue. One stood by the servant's entrance, and the others loitered at the busy street corner. Just as the sun disappeared, a new trio of guards trudged up the street to relieve them.

"How can anyone justify having city guards to protect their own house?" Ailuros wondered.

"Everything is for sale in Newport," Akke replied.

Their tea was delivered efficiently, and they were promptly left alone, the door to the café pulled shut against the deepening chill. They sat and watched the world go by, noting the first of the servants departing the manor house alongside the new guards settling in for their cold watch. The shops were just starting to close up for the night, although many pedestrians continued to stroll and browse. Half a block away, the dim frontage of the warehouse glistened from multiple 'accidental' spills of oil.

"Why did you pick that warehouse?" Ailuros asked. "It's not the largest this road has to offer."

"Have you noticed that every day the city guards who stand in front of the manor house also go into that warehouse?"

"I assumed it was part of their patrol duties, it being a city warehouse."

"Yes, but each one of them goes inside the warehouse at the end of his shift. Just for a few minutes, then comes out with a small sack."

Ailuros sipped his tea. "Some kind of extra payment?"

"Probably a little something extra for guarding their boss' house."

He nodded toward the trio of guards standing across the lane. "So, if it burns, they're going to be highly motivated to save it."

She raised her cup to him, downing the last of her tea.

New light flickered against the grey stone of the manor house. Raised voices drifted from the street behind them, and the new glow was joined by a sudden roar. Screams pierced the air, followed by shouts of alarm.

"Fire!"

Chaos erupted up and down the street. Pedestrians hurried as fast as their finery allowed away from the sudden inferno, while others removed from immediate danger were transfixed, their attention fully on the blaze. Shopkeepers scrambled to grab their wares, and a few brave souls even rushed in with heavy blankets, but they quickly backed away from the intense heat.

Across the lane, the three guards bolted toward the warehouse.

Akke was out of her seat, tossing coins on the table as she hurried up Lilac Lane. Ailuros was right behind her, and in their sudden haste they looked like any other wealthy citizens caught up in the drama.

Akke and Ailuros stepped into the shadows under the arch of the servants' entrance. The narrow alley was clear except for a pile of crates stacked to one side, several paces from the wooden door.

"Something to help you up," Akke said, nodding to the crates.

Ailuros scoffed, leaping in a single bound over the crates and nearly two man-heights up onto the wall. "Just try and keep up, witch."

He scrambled higher, disappearing over the crenelations in seconds. Akke stilled herself, listening carefully as footsteps approached the servants' door from the inside. Summoning her magic, she pressed herself against the wall facing the door.

Camouflage.

The door swung open as a servant pushed it with her shoulder, both hands hefting a tub of food scraps. Busy managing her heavy load, she walked right past Akke, who hid behind a clever illusion. It was a difficult spell that required some concentration to maintain. It didn't make her fully invisible; instead, it let her blend into the environment, her body taking on the monotone grey of the stone wall behind her. The servant struggled toward the archway to the street, not even glancing back.

Akke reached for the door as it started to close,

slowing it just enough for her to slip in.

The passageway inside was lit only by a candle mounted in a wall sconce, and Akke took a moment to let her spell adjust her appearance to match the new environment. Stepping forward softly, she listened for anyone else moving around. The Network hadn't been able to get her drawings of the interior of this house, but she figured all she had to do was find stairs leading upward.

She slipped past the doors to the kitchen and found herself looking into a grand dining hall, with wide stairs leading up at the far end. Two servants were laying new place settings for breakfast, one of them singing softly as they diligently went about their work. The only illumination came from the four candelabras standing along the table.

Akke felt the magic coursing through her as she concentrated on her spell, hoping it would be enough as she slowly moved along the closest wall of the dining hall. Her colour shifted to match the dark wood, her feet padding softly against the floor. One servant had her back to her as she laid cutlery along the near side of the table, and the other, although facing Akke, kept her gaze focused on the bowls as she placed them.

A floorboard squeaked under Akke's foot. She froze as the woman's eyes slowly rose. The servant's eyes stared blankly at Akke—no, stared through her—but the singing didn't falter. Akke very carefully released the breath she realized she was holding and continued to shuffle along the wall.

After what seemed an eternity, Akke reached the base of the staircase. With a final glance back at the two servants, she scurried up the stairs and got herself around the first landing. A few more steps and she was on the second floor in some sort of receiving room.

There was no obvious route upward, but in one corner of the deserted room she saw a closed door mounted in a wall that clearly curved—the tower. She was across the room in seconds, hand reaching for the door latch.

To her surprise, it was unlocked. With another glance around the receiving room, she pushed it open and slipped through.

The stone stairs spiralled upward into the darkness, with only a faint glow high above. There was always the risk that someone would be in the office when they struck, but she and Ailuros were ready for that. For now, she just had to get to the third floor.

A sound below her indicated someone had followed her up the stairs. Possibly one of the servants from the dining room, having finished their task. They didn't appear to be alerted to her presence: their footsteps slowly padded around the receiving room on the other side of the door, no doubt going about their duties. However, the strain of having to concentrate on her spell and listen to ensure she was not being followed almost cost Akke. She rounded the corner and nearly smacked into an older woman holding a candle, just in the process of closing a third-floor door.

Akke froze, bare inches from the woman's shoulder.

The woman turned sharply. "Who's there?"

Her candle swung around as she turned, forcing Akke to dodge sideways.

The movement was too quick for her spell to adapt, and the woman's eyes snapped toward the movement.

Akke raised her hand.

Sleep.

Catching the woman and her candleholder as she toppled, Akke set both down on the floor. The reflexive burst of casting the sleep spell made her head pound, and she lost concentration on her masking spell.

Akke stood in silence for a moment. Her heart thudded rapidly in her chest, but there was no indication that her brief encounter had been detected by anyone in the room below. So, she continued quietly onwards through the door from which the servant had just emerged.

Scanning the round landing, she determined which door she needed—the one facing away from the street—and tried it. The door was locked, but a quick search of the sleeping woman revealed a set of keys.

Akke unlocked the door, cracked it to peer into the quiet darkness, then moved inside. The window was clearly visible, with the glow of the fire outside shining through the clear glass. Akke double-checked that the room was unoccupied before trying to open the window. It was locked, and none of the keys she held fit the lock.

Glancing through the glass, she saw a pair of white paws gripping the stone frame below. Ailuros still wore his dark cloak to cover his fur, but as he hung on the wall the sleeves had fallen back.

Reaching under her own cloak, Akke pulled out her lock-picking tools and went to work. The device securing the window was fairly simple and took mere moments to disarm. Pushing the frame up, she leant out over the sill.

"Quit hanging around, cat-man," she whispered. "We have work to do."

"Your wit is worthy of a fourth-rate minstrel," he growled in reply.

Ailuros scrambled up the last of the wall and slithered through the window. With feline grace he rose to his feet, pulled his spear free and then idly dusted off his cloak.

"Do you need a moment to rest your limbs?" she asked.

"No, do you?"

Sighing, she locked the window and motioned him to follow. They left the room and hurried past the sleeping woman, ascending the next flight of stairs to find yet another locked door.

The stolen keys once against assisted them, but as Akke went to open the door, she turned to her friend. "Remember, something magical has taken down every thief who's broken into this room. Whatever's in there, I expect it to surprise us."

"Let me go first, witch," he said. "If I get taken down, then at least you'll see what it is."

She paused, recognizing the self-sacrifice in his easy words. "Well ... maybe I don't want you to get taken down."

He frowned. "We don't have time for this. You must survive. Ruthia is waiting for you, not me."

"But—"

"And neither that sleep spell, nor that fire are going to last for long. We have to keep moving."

He was right, of course. Damn, but why did feelings of guilt settle over her so easily now? Motioning him to the other side of the door, Akke huddled in close to the wall, reached over, and threw the door open.

When nothing happened, they both peeked in. In the flickering light reflecting from the burning warehouse, they saw an official's office complete with an ornate desk, a fine silk rug, and hand-carved chairs arranged for conversation. One wall was dedicated to towering shelves stuffed with books, scrolls, and sheaves of parchment. Nothing stirred except the door bouncing against its hinges.

Akke scanned for any tripwires or magic glyphs. "It looks clear," she said.

Ailuros stepped into the room, crouched and ready to spring. He stalked forward cautiously, gripping his spear. Akke moved in behind him, scanning all around. The ceiling was clear, and nothing moved on the shelves. She barely heard Ailuros' muffled footfalls on the rug as he tipped his spear toward the desk. Akke followed, appreciating that the softness of the rug beneath her own boots granted her total silence.

Then she sensed a faint shift of the air around her.

Ailuros shoved her backward with such force that she stumbled and fell. Even as she rolled back and to her feet, Ailuros leapt straight upward. But not before all four corners of the rug snapped upward and grabbed him.

Ailuros' spear punched down through the tightly woven material, but the magical rug didn't falter in grabbing the panthor and pulling him down. Releasing his spear, Ailuros lashed out with all four sets of claws, raking the rug as it enveloped him. Within seconds, he disappeared within its voluminous folds.

Akke yanked out both her daggers. She pounced, slicing at the writhing mass of silk. It was impossible to know if she was hitting her friend, but all that mattered was cutting a way through to him. She recalled only too clearly the fate of every other thief: death from suffocation.

As the *animated* rug pressed closer and closer around

Ailuros, she knew she only had seconds. She punched a dagger into a section of rug and pulled it taut, then slashed a long gap with her other dagger. Then she hooked another section and did the same. Then a third.

Following the last cut she spotted a flash of white fur, then teeth as Ailuros fought his way toward air. She grabbed the tear in the rug and heaved, slicing away with her blade to widen the hole. Ailuros got his head through, reaching both paws out to rip at the gash further. Now that he could breathe, Akke hacked away at other parts of the rug that still flailed in its mindless attack.

Finally, the rug sagged, its magical energy dissipating as it fell apart in tatters.

Ailuros crouched on all fours, taking long, deep breaths. Akke stayed on her feet, scanning the room for any new threats. After the pandemonium of the last few moments, the office was deathly quiet. But that wouldn't last; they'd already made far too much noise.

"Well," Ailuros said finally, "that's a new one."

Akke motioned him well clear, still eyeing the tattered mess. "Animated objects are nasty. No thought. No mercy. I can see how a single thief wouldn't have a chance."

"You were right that sticking together would give us the advantage. I appreciate you anew, witch."

She paused, noting the sincerity in his voice. He rose to his full height, but his huge eyes regarded her with respect.

She nodded to him. "You too," she said, rounding the ornate desk. "Now let's find that book and get out of here."

There were no mechanical traps rigged, and her tools made short work of the lock. She slid the drawer open and saw a simple, leather-bound book. Sensing no new magic around her, she picked it up. It was smaller than most books, easily held in one hand. In sheer curiosity she flipped it open, scanning a few pages of dates, locations, and cargo.

"They wanted us to steal a shipping schedule?" she wondered aloud.

A shout from the lobby below announced that someone had found the sleeping servant. Akke and Ailuros exchanged a glance. A white panthor and elf must not be seen at the scene of the crime.

"Who cares," Ailuros said, already scanning out the window. "Let's go."

Akke summoned her magic, aiming for the door and the stairs leading down to the floor below.

Darkness.

New shouts of alarm were followed by a loud thump, followed by cursing. It would take the guards time to feel their way through that mess.

Pocketing the book, she went to work on the window's lock. When it clicked open Ailuros slid over the sill, gripping the rough stone, and working his way down.

Akke reached into her belt pocket and grabbed a glob of magical sticky wax, pressing it against the outside wall just below the window. Pulling out her wire rope, she pressed one end into the wax and let the other end drop. It wasn't long enough to reach the bottom of the tower, but it was good enough. Climbing out the window, she wrapped one arm around the rope and pressed her feet tight against it. In a controlled slide she descended the tower, dropping the last five feet to the stone terrace.

The fire was still burning a half-block away, but the flames were sullen and in retreat. In the dancing shadows Akke and Ailuros ran to the crenels at the back of the manor house. The street below bustled with activity; more city guards had arrived, and even more citizens had spilled out onto the street to witness the commotion.

Making their escape along the streets was too risky. It would only take one witness to spot Ailuros' white fur and potentially link the duo to the crime. Akke motioned for Ailuros to climb up the neighbouring building, which pressed in close to the manor house. The panthor easily scaled the wall and then reached down to haul her up. Together they fled along the rooftops of Lilac Lane.

CHAPTER 7

The sitting room of Patrick's house was flooded in warm candelabra light that banished the dark chill of late winter. Akke had already requested that Patrick send word to Costa to arrange a meeting with the Guild. Now there was nothing to do but wait.

And, of course, study this book.

"It's like we thought," she mused, flipping another page. "It's a list of Pellio's shipments. Past, present, and future, arriving and leaving Newport."

"Perhaps the Guild wants to rob some of these shipments," Ailuros offered. "They are thieves, after all."

"Well, there's certainly enough wealthy cargos here to make it worth their while."

"Although, would Pellio not just change all the dates if he knows this book has been compromised?"

Akke flipped another page. "For the departures, yes. But the arrivals will have been pre-arranged weeks or months in advance—you can't tell a ship on the high seas to change its schedule unless you're willing to spend a fortune in *sending* spells If the Guild is looking to hurt him, the price of all that magic would eat into his profits, and Pellio's reputation of delivering goods on time would surely suffer. Maybe they plan on selling similar goods that will hit the market in the absence of timely competition ... Whatever the case, it's not our concern."

Ailuros muttered an acknowledgement, but Akke barely heard him. Her eyes were riveted to the pages in front of her, detailing a list of past 'special' shipments, scheduled irregularly every few months. But only one future shipment was logged: due to leave tomorrow morning on the dawn tide. Oddly, it was leaving from a village to the north that was known to be abandoned, at least when she'd lived in Newport. Too many goblin raids if she remembered correctly.

That in itself was strange, and suggested a transaction best not viewed by officials, but it was the cargo that caught her eye. The product being shipped was divided into colour and age, and was something called ...

"*Abeed* ..." she said out loud, trying to figure out the word.

The great feline head in her peripheral snapped up.

She glanced at him. "Do you know what that word means?"

"Yes," he growled, "it's perhaps the most hated word amongst my people. It's from the tongue of Khasiba, and it means 'slave.'"

Despite the candles around her, Akke went cold. "Pellio is dealing in the slave trade," she said, showing Ailuros the pages.

His lips curled back to reveal dagger teeth. "Then we will tear him to pieces."

Akke was silent, momentarily gripped by indecision. There were a half-dozen entries spanning back over the last couple years. Her heart sank for all those poor souls, but this was the value of the favour she had promised.

Whether to expose Pellio or exploit him, it mattered not. This was the reason the Guild had sent her after a simple shipment log. Upsetting that now would cost her Ruthia's own freedom.

A soft growl snapped her out of her reverie. Turning, she looked into Ailuros' eyes to see the anger and pain there. She could not let Ruthia down. Not now that she was so close. But she would rather burn in the thirteen layers of the Abyss than fail Ailuros as well. She made her decision. "We will," she said firmly. "After we hand this over."

She cut off his snarl of protest. "I never said we would let them profit from it." She was already reaching for a page of parchment and fresh ink. "Once we secure Ruthia, we will ensure this shipment is stopped." She would figure out how to deal with double-crossing the Guild after they had done what's right. And after Ruthia was safe.

She started copying down the dates and locations of each of the past shipments as well as the next. "Because you're right, we have to stop this."

Ailuros leant in close to read over her shoulder. "That one is tomorrow."

"I know." She sighed. "Do you think we can get that far out of the city in one night?"

Ailuros' claws tapped small nicks into the desk. "I could, witch." He looked out at the rising moon. "But a shipment like that would be heavily guarded. I don't know if I would be able free them alone." There was humility in his voice, but determination as well. He was prepared to go alone if he had to. "Without a mount, you won't be able to keep up."

"Okay, let's move quickly then. We can figure out the

details after we secure Ruthia. Even if we have to steal a horse."

Just as she rose to her feet, Patrick strolled into the room. He paused, reading the tension in the air, but met her eyes fearlessly. "Costa has arranged your meeting with the Guild," he said, watching both his agitated guests carefully. "You can go to his residence, and he'll take you from there."

Akke paused, thinking quickly. The slave trade was an awful reality in the underbelly of Newport, as much as every official statement condemned it. But was the Network as an organization opposed to it?

She glanced around the opulent room she was in. Slavery was big business, and those willing to engage in it got very, very rich. Would she find support for their actions within the Network? While alienating the Thieves' Guild and a merchant prince like Pellio?

Not very likely.

"I can arrange a carriage for you," Patrick said, gesturing toward the door.

"No thanks," she said, ensuring her daggers were still on her belt. "It's best if we go silently." She slung her quiver of arrows over her back and grabbed her bow while donning her trademark, wide-brimmed hat with its sewn-in metal skull cap.

"As you wish," he said, stepping out of the way as she and Ailuros strode through.

They said nothing as they descended the stairs into the cellar, marched through the underground tunnels, and emerged in the guardhouse across the street. She barely glanced at the sentries who greeted them and let them pass. It wasn't until the cold night air slapped her across the face that she finally slowed.

Ailuros padded closer. "Why did we not accept Patrick's offer? Surely if your Network has helped thus far, they could now."

"Not if they're part of it," she hissed. "First rule of Newport: don't trust anyone." They were practically running down the street now, but Akke didn't care. They needed to get this exchange with the Guild completed and to get Ruthia.

"This really is a vile place," he commented, keeping pace with her.

Akke knew she had to stay in control. Emotions were not her friends right now. But too many memories of life on these streets welled up within her. Too many times she'd been shoved down by the powerful. Or her friends had suffered at the whims of a bully. Too many promising lives wasted in petty squabbles. She had to get Ruthia out and leave this wretched city behind her.

It didn't take long for them reach Costa's manor where his four-horsed carriage was already prepped in the courtyard. From the driver's bench, a figure raised a cocked crossbow. Diana, Costa's bodyguard.

Akke slowed, raising her hands. "Peace, Diana. We're here for our ride."

The woman lowered her weapon and gestured for them to climb inside. "Did you run the whole way here?"

Akke realized she was puffing for breath. "Maybe."

A flash of respect crossed Diana's face as she took up the reins.

Akke opened the door to the carriage and climbed in, sliding over for Ailuros to join her.

Costa was seated across from them, and he offered a polite nod. "My friends, welcome."

Costa was as flamboyant as ever with a red silk shirt and his jewel-encrusted scabbard fastened to the broad belt at his hip. His hair was mostly tied back in a practical ponytail, but a few strands fell loose to frame his handsome face.

Akke settled back in the seat as the carriage jerked into motion. "Thank you for arranging this meeting, Master Costa."

He smiled, his features softening. "There's no need for such formality ... Akke. I'm glad I can facilitate."

Despite the tension coursing through her, she felt herself relax. She knew better than to trust Costa, but she sensed neither malice nor deception in him. He just seemed genuinely interested in watching events unfold—and, if he could, profit along the way.

The ride through the deserted streets was swift and short, and within minutes the carriage clattered to a stop outside a nondescript, unlit building near the grand market.

The wooden frame creaked as Diana climbed down from her seat and then opened the door. "It's clear," she announced.

Ailuros was first out, head moving back and forth as he conducted his own scan. Akke heard him take a deep breath through his powerful nose. Only then did he nod up to her. She climbed down to the street, examining the dark buildings all around them. There were no lights in windows, no distant flickers of fires in hearths. The street was so dark that the skies above were awash in stars. Akke took advantage of her elven night vision to see what the humans couldn't, and confirmed that there were no surprises in the shadows.

"In here," Costa said as he reached for the door leading into the nearest building.

Akke gripped her bow and nocked an arrow, leaving the tension off the string. She followed Costa into the gloom of the building, her night vision making out what looked like a warehouse cluttered with sacks and crates. A single figure stood in the centre, cloaked and shrouded in a complete darkness that not even her elven eyes could pierce.

A moment later, bright light illuminated her section of the warehouse as someone un-shuttered a lantern, blinding her and her companions while further obscuring those behind its source. From the same direction she heard the tiny squeaks of wood as hidden figures shifted their positions. Hefting weapons, she assumed.

"My friends," Costa greeted amiably, apparently not the least bit intimidated as he stepped forward, "we come in peace."

"Master Costa," came the silken voice that Akke recognized as the elf, "you are always a man of your word."

Akke slipped her arrow into her bow hand, stepped forward, and thrust out the book. "And I'm a woman of mine. Here's the book you wanted."

The elf stepped forward, his long legs so graceful he practically glided toward her. His features were as timeless as any elf's, with a narrow, pointed face framed with golden hair that hung straight past his shoulders. His ice blue eyes bore into her.

But Akke wasn't charmed by the fey folk the way

humans were, and she saw past the ephemeral beauty to the darker soul within. This elf was old and disconnected from his woodland heritage by too many centuries amidst brick and stone. Weariness lined his features, brought not by physical exertion, but from the emotional toil of living as an elf in a human world.

A slender hand reached out to take the book from her fingers. He opened it, flipping through the pages. "I trust you did not take anything from it?"

"It's all there, isn't it?" Akke said, a little too defensively.

The elf snapped the book closed. "That's not the only way something can be taken."

The creak of movement all around her indicated weapons were being pointed at her, but she stood her ground.

"That is not the deal we made! You never said anything about not reading the book. Give me Ruthia, as promised, and let me go. I have no intention of interfering with the Guild."

Akke was sweating despite the chill; she instantly regretted her outburst. Had she just compromised Ruthia's safety? She needed to get her emotions under control. She was so close.

A long moment passed, the tableau in the warehouse frozen in place. Akke listened for any movement around her—even the rustle of a finger on a crossbow trigger—and heard nothing. Every person in this room was a dangerous killer, and any action would bring consequences. She stared nervously at the elf. He stared back.

"Perhaps," Costa said quietly, "we could all take a step back. None of us are enemies."

"Very well, *charfirya*," the elf said almost absently, still staring into her eyes. "You play a dangerous game, but the Guild will not press the point."

The elf gestured dismissively with both hands. Akke heard crossbows being lowered. He stepped back, bowing slightly. "The Guild will not interfere with anything you choose to do tonight, Akke of Sanctuary."

"Wait a minute!" Akke snapped. "What about Ruthia? Are you a man of your word?"

The elf stopped just at the edge of the light. "Your pet was taken from the Serpents in a raid earlier today," he said, "by attackers we know well."

"By who?" Akke demanded. But she didn't need to guess. The sinking feeling in her gut told her exactly who.

"It seems Pellio is aware of your quest to free your pet, and I suspect you know precisely where she is now bound."

Akke nodded slowly, her body going numb. She had failed.

"Where?" Costa still sounded wary.

When Akke didn't respond, Ailuros growled, "The merchant deals in slaves."

Beside her, Akke sensed Costa stiffen.

"It's true," she said. "The book proves it. Pellio has been selling slaves, and he's arranging another shipment tomorrow morning."

"Pellio's indiscretions are none of the Guild's business," the elf said. "But by moving openly against us, he has broken the truce that has kept the bloodshed off the streets between our factions. The Guild revokes all protection afforded to him and his concerns." His eyes flicked to Costa. "Anyone acting against him on this night is immune to our wrath and will not lose our favour."

"Understood," Costa growled.

"Track those slaves down, Akke of Sanctuary, and you shall have your prize." The elf retreated into the shadows. "May Salina guide you this night."

Akke knew the gods were real, but she'd never depended on them; she'd always made her own luck.

And so, she would tonight, too. She wasn't going to give up. There were other ways to make it out of the city in time.

She left the warehouse and made for the four-horse carriage.

"Costa," she said, "can I borrow your ride? I will owe you a favour."

"No," he said, keeping pace. "I'm coming with you."

Costa's surprise insistence of joining her would normally have set her paranoia on edge. But the pressure of the situation and time-sensitive nature of her quest overrode her usual caution. Besides, Costa had a reputation as a seasoned adventurer, and he had kept his word up till now. Only the gods knew what they would be facing when they caught up with the slavers.

Ailuros gave her a simple nod of approval. Glancing at Costa's *kilij* at his waist and Diana's twin swords at hers, Akke knew accepting any assistance at this stage was the wisest course of action.

Akke climbed up onto the driver's bench, sliding over as Diana climbed up behind her. "You drive," Akke said, shouldering her bow and hefting Diana's crossbow. "I'll shoot."

Akke described their destination as the Costa and Ailuros clambered in as well. The carriage door slammed shut behind them; Costa thumped twice on the ceiling; Diana cracked the reins; and the horses leapt into motion.

The deserted streets flew past as the carriage clattered over the cobbles, the breeze cold enough that Akke had to pull her cloak taut. Diana's black hair fluttered in the breeze as she expertly steered the carriage around corners of back alleys toward the wide boulevard of North Road.

Soon enough, the city's northern gates loomed ahead. Diana slowed, calling out to the night guards. "Make way!"

An elderly guard stepped into the road, forcing Diana to rein in.

"We're not supposed to open the gates after nightfall to anyone but authorized travellers," he said. It was a well-practiced sentence, and he practically had his hand up already, awaiting payment.

Akke fumbled to reach for her purse, but Diana was already flipping him a coin. In the torch light Akke saw the clear flash of a silver eagle. The guard stared dumbfounded at it for a moment after he caught it.

"I'm sure you'll agree," Diana called, "that everything is in order."

"Yes, yes, good lady. Open the gates!"

As the heavy doors creaked open, Diana flicked the reins anew and the carriage started rolling.

"A bit of an expensive bribe," Akke whispered as they passed through the gate.

"Enough to ensure absolutely no delays," Diana

replied, her eyes on the dark road.

Akke appreciated that, but she was mystified as well. The carriage gained speed. The moon was low and huge in the sky, providing just enough light for her human driver to see the contrast of the stone road against the darker countryside.

"But why?" she asked finally. "Why are you helping me?"

"Costa would have it no other way," Diana replied.

"I take it he opposes slavery?"

For a moment Diana was silent as she leant into the wind, hair flying behind her. "I suppose you could say that."

The first few miles beyond the city walls were marked by the lights of many hamlets and villages, acting as waypoints to navigate by. But soon, as the trade road continued north, these gave way to the uncivilised wilderness. They rode for hours, pushing the horses faster than they should have in the darkness. Thankfully, the moon and cloudless night provided some dim light, even so Akke used her elven vision to occasionally help guide Diana.

As the first grey light of false dawn illuminated the eastern horizon, the low shapes of dilapidated buildings began to stand out against the faintly glimmering sea. Diana slowed, manoeuvring into the narrow, dirt roads of the abandoned village.

"There's a bunch of docks up ahead," Akke reported. "Some rowboats are on approach and a larger ship is at anchor, past the breakers of the harbour."

"That's where we're headed," Diana replied, steering the horses down onto the low, grassy slope beyond the houses.

Akke bent down, rapping on the carriage door. "We're here, and the transfer looks to be occurring soon. Get ready!"

"Ready and waiting," came Costa's reply, echoed by a snarl from Ailuros.

In the dim light, Akke could see a large wagon hitched to two horses standing near the dock. Just ahead of it was a smaller, more comfortable carriage. There were a half-dozen men around the wagon. Even from this distance she could tell the men were armed. Most of them were looking out to where the rowboats were making their final approach. The noise of the breakers and general activity around the dock thankfully covered her own carriage's approach.

The wagon they guarded looked like a prisoner transport; a heavy chain barred a single door, concealing the true cargo inside. Akke's blood boiled at the thought of Ruthia and a half-dozen others packed together in the slave wagon.

In most situations, it was best to talk things out, but Akke was beyond talking. They were outnumbered and had to take every advantage they could get.

If human, the guards wouldn't be able to see her clearly yet, but she could see them just fine. She raised the crossbow and fired. The first man dropped without a sound. His companion turned in shock.

"Attackers!" another shouted.

Akke dropped the crossbow and pulled out her bow, reaching for an arrow just as she saw a tall man in robes step out from behind the well-appointed carriage, already gesturing as he performed a spell.

"Oh, sh—"

Their carriage exploded in flames. Akke flew through the air on a wave of heat, barely clinging to her bow as she crashed to the ground. Their horses shrieked as they fell, the flaming carriage coming to rest in a shattered heap.

Akke saw a nimble form leap clear and then a flash of white fur through the smoke. Diana hit the ground not far away, rolling in the dirt as she desperately tried to put out the flames engulfing her. Costa was nowhere to be seen.

A couple of thugs came to inspect the burning carnage, waving smoke from their eyes. They never saw Ailuros leaping down on them. Most of his white fur was badly singed, and angry pink skin was exposed in ragged patches where he was burnt. But his spear struck with devastating efficiency.

Akke's eyes still stung with smoke. Flames spun round her. Her cloak was on fire she realized. Cursing, she shed the burning cloak and ran for cover as crossbow bolts whistled past her.

A collapsed fishing hut was all she could reach, but not before a bolt slammed into the gambeson padding on her flank. The armour was sufficient to absorb most of the hit, but part of the bolt's head made it through to pierce her flesh.

Ignoring the sudden pain, she pulled the shaft free, took a firing position and loosed her own arrow. It thudded into the corner of the slave wagon but was enough to force her attacker to seek cover.

Pulling off her quiver and placing it in front of her, she grabbed another arrow and sought a target. A head peeked around the wagon. She released the string. This arrow also soared wide, trailing smoke behind it. She stared down at her quiver and realized that it, too, was smouldering.

Dumping out her arrows, she spread them out and looked for undamaged ones. Most of the fletchings were badly burnt. Without them, her arrows would be much harder to aim.

Another bolt struck the low wall in front of her. She grabbed the best arrow and crouched down, peeking over the edge with her bow. Spying the crossbowman, who was using the wagon as cover to reload his weapon, Akke channelled her magic and projected the sound of feet rushing the thug's position.

As the crossbowman exposed himself to fire at the non-existent charge, she loosed the bowstring. The arrow struck him in the face. He fell backward, dead before he could hit the ground.

More shouts indicated new enemies running up the dock—one of the rowboats had unloaded its sailors. Beyond, the second rowboat was closing fast. Akke grabbed a burnt arrow and fired at the dock, then grabbed another and repeated. At this range and with her damaged ammunition there was no way her shots would strike anyone, but maybe the sudden rain of arrows would force them down.

Sure enough, the newcomers scattered for cover as her first arrow struck the jetty. She fired three more, then gripped her bow and a few blackened arrows. She ran toward the slave wagon.

Diana backed into view, both hands wielding short swords that deftly fended off a pair of goons. The men hacked and slashed with furious imprecision, and Diana fended off the blows expertly.

As she approached, Akke could see that Diana was hurt. The woman's armour was charred from the fireball, and the skin visible on her exposed arms and legs was red and raw. Even through her pain, though, Diana saw Akke approaching and deftly side-stepped away, drawing her attackers to turn their backs on Akke.

Akke dropped her bow and buried her daggers into the back of the first goon, twisting them and wrenching them free. A torrent of blood followed her blades as she turned to the next enemy, but Diana's free sword plunged under his guard to bury itself up and behind his ribcage. He gargled once, weapon falling from lifeless fingers.

"Thanks," Diana gasped.

Akke looked towards the dock in time to see Ailuros finishing another opponent and begin his charge on the wizard. His singed fur was now stained red but, as always, she couldn't tell whose blood it was. The panthor snarled and ran forward. That was when Akke felt another crackle of magic.

Ailuros froze in position, toppling helplessly face-first into the grass. Akke saw Pellio's wizard glaring in grim satisfaction. Beside him were three men. One was Cinderblock, the thug from the casino, his stupid face lit up in laughter at the sight of Ailuros immobilized by a *hold* spell. He and his men lumbered forward, raising their swords for a *coup de grace*.

From atop the slave wagon, the heavy form of Costa suddenly leapt down, felling two goons in as many slashes and finally knocking Cinderblock's sword clear as the two men crashed to the ground, Costa on top. Costa's curved blade danced in the air as he smashed the pommel into Cinderblock's head, but the giant man grabbed Costa and hurled him aside. Costa landed heavily but regained his feet before Cinderblock could fully rise.

Akke realized Costa was wearing nothing but his leggings, his heavy belt, and his smouldering boots, his skin raw from recent burns. He limped slightly as he closed on Cinderblock again, but his muscles rippled as that curved sword swung in anticipation.

Cinderblock looked between his advancing opponent and the helpless panthor. His square chin shifted back and forth as he tried to figure out what to do next.

"Kill the panthor!" the wizard screamed.

Cinderblock hesitated, lifting his sword to block Costa's mighty swing. The blades clanged together in the morning air.

The wizard gestured in another spell, and a *firebolt* sizzled through the air at Costa. The big man winced at the explosive impact but didn't falter, slashing down at Cinderblock again.

The wizard fired two more *firebolts* in quick succession, each mini detonation hitting Costa's unprotected skin. Akke could see they had an effect, but not the effect she expected. Orange runes glowed across his *kilij's* blade. Costa was far more prepared than he seemed, Akke realized.

The wizard briefly retreated into cover as he screamed orders, his frustration over his failed attempts to kill Costa obvious. From the jetty, more sailors rushed forward, swords up. The bulk of those sailors rushed to aid Cinderblock, but the wizard directed three others to advance on Akke's position.

"Help Costa!" Akke shouted to Diana, running beside

her. "I'll take the wizard."

"On it." Diana raised her swords and closed in on the fray.

Costa was already on the attack, his *kilij* slashing through unarmoured bodies as sailors came to Cinderblock's assistance. Blood dripped down his back, but together with Diana they were holding their own and keeping Ailuros safe.

Akke didn't have time to marvel at their swordsmanship as she reached the back of the wagon. The three goons were still closing as she lined up her shot. The smoking arrow flew wide but was enough to send them all diving for cover again. She ran around the wagon, trying to get a better angle on the wizard, and then fired a second shot from behind the hobbled horses. This one punched into the stomach of one of the goons, taking him out of the fight.

Akke reached the skittish horses and ducked down, peering out at the wizard, who was preparing another spell on the carriage steps.

In desperation, she prayed for a blessing from Salina. And aimed her final arrow.

It sailed true enough, hitting the wizard's chest and interrupting his spellcasting. But instead of penetrating, the arrow deflected, tearing fabric and leaving only a superficial wound in its wake.

Mage armour. She cursed under her breath. It would require a more powerful blow to kill this wizard.

Akke dropped her bow and advanced, daggers out. The wizard was screaming at his men to rush her position. It was a simple tactic: tie her up in melee while he prepared another spell to disable her.

One of the thugs roared as he advanced. Akke recognized his voice: Blade. She snarled. That little bastard had sold her out, sold Ruthia out, and was on board with selling slaves. He was going to pay.

She quickly assessed her options. Ailuros was still frozen, struggling to shake off the *hold* spell. Costa and Diana's battle to defend him against Cinderblock and his allies was growing desperate. They were in real danger of being overrun, and she could expect no help from their quarter. Blade and his partner were almost upon her, and the wizard was preparing to cast another spell.

She could try and *sleep* Blade and his flunky, but in that time the wizard would have free rein to cast his own spell at her. She needed to buy more time. She needed something special.

She had only ever cast this spell in practice under Magister Abarax's tutelage. She desperately hoped it worked as she whispered her own brief incantation.

Mirror Image.

Three more Akkes suddenly sprung from her body, daggers in their hands. Her opponents were confused, and even the wizard paused his spellcasting to re-assess. If he wanted to hit Akke, he needed to know which "her" was the correct target, or he risked wasting the spell.

Shouts of alarm went up as the goons paused their advance, raising weapons to defend against this sudden threat. Akke pressed her advantage. All of her mirror images also advanced as one, swinging their daggers as she did.

Blade's eyes snapped around at the four Akkes before

him. She closed in on him with murder in her eyes, knowing her mirrors did the same.

Blade grimaced in frustration, backing up and looking to the wizard for guidance. The wizard glared in frustration as he tried to identify the real Akke. Then he lashed out with a sudden spell.

A spray of three *scorching rays* rocketed through the air, each a bright streak of concentrated flame, shooting towards a different image of Akke. She rolled, barely dodging one ray of intense heat that passed over her to hit the mirrored image behind her.

She heard the thunder of approaching footsteps and rolled to her feet just in time to plunge a dagger into the confused thug accompanying Blade.

In the silence that followed the *scorching rays*, Akke realized that her *mirror images* had all been struck. She was exposed once again.

"Kill her!" the wizard screamed.

Blade flourished his sword and advanced. "Let's finish this, bitch."

She charged forward. Her magic was already drained from the heist that evening, and she knew she was down to her very last spell. Screaming in a sudden fury that shook off her fatigue, she unleashed the last of her magic.

Sleep.

Blade slumped to one knee ... but resisted the full effects of the spell. His sword came up in a frantic, weakened defence.

She knocked it aside with one dagger as her other stabbed beneath. He was slow to dodge, and the blade sliced across his face, opening a large gash. He toppled backward as she lunged to finish the job.

The *sleep* spell's effect, however, was already wearing off, and with sudden vigour Blade's sword swung upward, knocking her left dagger from her hand.

Her whole body slammed into his as they hit the ground. Her knee found his crotch, and her right dagger slashed at his sword arm. He kept his grip on his sword and punched her with his free hand as blood flowed down his face and arm.

Her dagger stabbed down into his shoulder, coating her blade in more of his blood. But before she could twist to do more damage, she felt something cold and hard slam against the side of her head and she fell off him, vision fading.

She lifted her dagger instinctively in defence but was too slow. The sword descended onto her head ... only to clang off the metal skullcap sewn into the expensive fabric of her broad-brimmed hat.

A second slash went low, catching her across the ribs. The blade sliced through her armour, but enough of the blow was absorbed by her gambeson to leave only a shallow cut.

Blade was on his knees, gasping in pain and bleeding from multiple wounds, but he swung again. She rolled backward, finding her other dagger in the grass. Blade struggled to his feet, face bloody and pale.

"Get out of the way you fool!" the wizard cried.

Blade staggered clear. The wizard raised his hand in arcane gestures, a look of victory plastered on his face.

Only for it to turn to a grimace of agony as a spear flew through the air, impaling his thigh. His *firebolt* spell went wide, detonating on the slave wagon behind Akke. The fire sizzled against the tar-sealed wood and smoke began to rise. Akke could just make out screams from inside.

The wizard staggered. The spear slipped loose in a torrent of blood as he wrenched it free. "Get me out of here!" Panic and pain fuelled the wizard's cries.

Blade looked down at Akke with pure hatred, then staggered away to hook the wizard's arm over his shoulders and rush for the docks.

Ailuros, having freed himself from the *hold* spell, moved to defend the weakened Costa and Diana, snatching up a dead sailor's cutlass and hacking away with savage abandon. As she watched, Cinderblock finally broke through Diana's exhausted defence, his sword stabbing into her torso.

Every part of Akke's body was screaming at her, but she staggered to her knees. The smoke against the wagon was thickening.

"To me, you imbecile!" the wizard shouted. "To me!"

With a final, mighty swing of his sword that knocked Costa back on his heels, Cinderblock turned and ran for the fleeing wizard, leaving his remaining allies to hold off Costa and the panthor.

Ailuros quickly killed another sailor as Costa finished off the last two. Ailuros leapt in pursuit of the retreating Cinderblock. His feline speed was more than enough to overtake the fleeing men. But even in his wounded state, the wizard had one final spell in reserve to help cover his retreat.

Four streaks of arcane energy spiralled through the air. No matter how much Ailuros tried to turn and dodge, the *magic missiles* arched to follow, eventually colliding with his burnt torso and sending him sprawling to the ground, wracked with pain.

Akke contemplated joining the chase, but Cinderblock and Blade were already hauling the wizard into one the docked rowboats. Besides, the screams of fright and rising heat behind her drew her full attention. She raced towards the wagon. The wagon was locked, and smoke was starting to fill the interior. Akke reached for her pouch with her lockpicks. Gone. She must have lost it in the battle. Panic threatened to overwhelm her as she desperately slammed the butt of her dagger against the lock, cursing the loss of her tools. It didn't budge. Behind the wooden doors, terrified voices begged her to open the door.

Looking up desperately, she saw Costa feeding a potion down the fallen Diana's throat. He sensed Akke's gaze, assessing the new danger instantly. Akke slammed her hilt into the lock again, but it didn't budge.

Costa rose from Diana and grabbed his magical *kilij*. As he ran forward, he motioned Akke clear. "Get back from the door!" he shouted.

His blade slammed into the chain, shattering it like ice and burying itself in the wood beyond. He wrenched it free and pulled at the broken chain.

Akke grabbed the doors and threw them open. "This way!"

Costa was already retreating, sprinting to the fallen Ailuros, pulling another wooden vial from his belt to render assistance.

A small crowd of young girls scrambled to jump down

from the wagon. Akke hustled them forward to make room for the next. All the while her eyes searched desperately for blonde, curly locks. Within moments the wagon was empty, and a group of seven terrified girls huddled together several paces away.

Akke assessed the situation from their point of view. Amidst a sea of bodies, the only movement that could be seen was a huge, powerful man with no shirt, burnt skin, and a wicked curved sword in his hand, bent over a blood-spattered beast. Then she looked at herself. A smoke-blackened elf in a bloody, tattered gambeson holding two dripping daggers. They hardly looked like saviours.

She slipped her daggers into their sheaths as she turned to face the girls. Raising her empty hands, she tried to smile. "It's okay," she said. "We're here to free you."

Her voice was hoarse, and she tasted blood in her mouth. Quickly dropping her smile for fear it might terrify them more, she took another slow step forward. "Is ..." She was almost afraid to ask. "Is there a girl named Ruthia with you?"

The girls shuffled uncertainly. Then a short, slight form emerged from the middle of the pack. She was about thirteen summers, the first curves on womanhood filling out her clothes. She stepped forward, eyeing Akke curiously. "Do I know you?" she asked in a small voice.

Her hair was tied back tight, and not as golden as it had once been, but Akke recognized the high cheekbones and wide, green eyes of the girl she'd once known.

Fighting back sudden tears, Akke took another step forward. "A long time ago," she said softly, "I made a promise that I'd come and find you. And that we'd leave Newport together."

Tears trickled down her cheeks, and she dropped to her knees in front of the girl. "I'm just so sorry it took me this long to keep my promise."

Ruthia stared at her, the light of recognition finally shining in her eyes. "Akke?" she whispered.

Akke nodded, suddenly unable to speak.

CHAPTER 8

The sun shone down with surprising warmth, and Akke felt no need to close the new, drab cloak she wore. The dockside crowds before her manoeuvred around the unmistakable form of a covered wagon from Costa's Curios. The rounded, wooden top was painted in gaudy colours and stood out among the dull browns and greys of the port.

Akke watched as two of Costa's men took positions off to the side, far enough to offer privacy, but close enough to come to their master's aid if need be. These two replacement bodyguards emphasized Diana's absence, a reminder of their near brush with death. Akke's eyes were quickly drawn back to Costa himself as he strode toward her. Coming to see her off.

His usually flamboyant colours were discarded for a brown cloak with a plain, but low-cut, linen shirt that mostly hid his singed chest.

"Diana?" Akke asked, genuinely concerned.

"She'll be okay," he replied. "My healers assure me she'll make a full recovery."

"Thank the gods you had those potions, though," Akke replied.

Costa let out a long, slow breath as he cast his gaze around the Newport docks. "It was a close thing," he said quietly. Then his usual grin emerged, and his eyes brightened. "You're an interesting woman, Akke, and I sense being near you brings interesting times."

She couldn't help but smile. Even bruised and battered, she felt like this man truly saw her. And she appreciated it.

"Have all the girls decided to go with you?" he asked.

"I've made the offer." She looked back over her shoulder to where *Fortune's Caress* was preparing to sail. "They're each deciding for themselves, but I have hope—I think Ruthia's excitement is infectious."

They'd all ridden back to Newport in the carriage abandoned by Pellio's wizard. It had been a tight squeeze to fit all seven freed girls into the main cabin with Akke and the unconscious Diana, but the ride had been mercifully smooth. During the ride, Akke had told Ruthia and the others a bit about her adventures of the past few years and offered them the chance to join her in Fairhaven. She'd given them all the freedom to choose, and to stay in Newport if they wanted.

Every single one of them had chosen Fairhaven.

"If any wish it, I can find them work," Costa offered. "But I doubt it'll be needed. I'm sure you're an inspiration to them."

"I hope I can be." Her eyes turned back to the rough warehouses and narrow streets leading up into the city. "I know what it is to be helpless on these streets. I want to offer them something better."

"You've already saved them," Costa said with sudden intensity, stepping in to grip her shoulders. "You saved them from a life of slavery."

His chest beneath the cloak was singed from the

fireball, but even through the reddened skin Akke could see an old scar. No, she realized suddenly, not a scar—a brand. The symbol of his own slavery forever preserved in his skin.

"*We* saved them," she insisted. "And now I can give them a chance at a decent life."

They stood together in silence as the crowds moved past them.

"And you're going to Fairhaven." It was a more of a statement then a question.

"That's my home."

She had already held up Regwald with her quest. His newly acquired goods bound for the Free Coast were woefully behind schedule, but Akke didn't feel safe traveling on any other ship with her own precious cargo.

She looked up at him again. "You should visit sometime. See what a fair city really is."

"I'd like that," he replied, meeting her gaze with a smile.

She would too, she knew, but she wasn't ready to say so yet. Instead, she looked out at the distant towers of Newport. "What are you going to do about Pellio?" she whispered.

He sighed, leading her onto the dock and away from the crowds. "The Guild spoke the truth: by openly attacking the Serpents, Pellio broke the treaty that keeps violence from spilling onto the street between the factions. That puts him in a very difficult position." His face was suddenly thoughtful. "And opens up new opportunities."

Akke was familiar enough with the unwritten rules that governed the street of Newport. In essence, the factions were free to act against each other's concerns as long as there was no open violence. Spilling blood on the street was bad for business in a city that thrived on trade.

Akke snorted, eliciting a twinge from her flank where one of her many wounds needed care. "Surely the authorities can shut him down," she protested, "now that we know he was dealing in slaves!"

"Pellio wasn't there," Costa countered. "He'll just claim that his underlings were working against his interests."

"And the evidence from the book?"

"Is just ink on paper. He'll denounce it as a fraudulent document created to besmirch his impeccable character."

"And the city will believe that?"

"Each councillor has used the same defence many times."

Her anger flared, but it was fleeting. She was leaving Newport, and honestly didn't care about its internal schemes and plots. She knew enough about the world to know that powerful men like Pellio rarely got what they deserved.

But even as her anger faded, a new worry welled up within her. "Will Pellio seek retribution against you?" she asked, slipping her hand onto his waist protectively.

"Word is already spreading that I'm the hero who rescued the slaves and removed the filth from his organisation."

"Really?" she said with sudden amusement. "That was fast."

"I don't waste time," he said with a wink. "He who speaks first controls the narrative."

"So, if he retaliates against you," she said as she

thought his plan through, "he's implicating himself."

"Pellio will have no choice but to *thank* me." His grin was decidedly smug.

"Well," she said after a moment, "the ship is going to sail soon. Favourable tides, and all that."

He nodded, then reached into one of the pockets of his cloak. He pulled out a small, wooden box that was secured with a single latch.

"I know you don't have the best memories of Newport. Please take this as a token to remind you that not everything here is wretched."

She took it, curious to open it but unable to take her eyes off the sincerity glowing from his handsome face. He grinned anew, then swept up one of her hands to place a gentle kiss on her knuckles. "Farewell, god-slayer and freer of slaves. I look forward to our next meeting."

He released her hand and turned, striding back to the colourful wagon that bore his name. He climbed up next to the driver with a flourish and tossed her a carefree wave as the wagon rolled into motion. She watched him until he disappeared around the corner.

Costa was a dangerous man, an opportunist, a scoundrel and, if the stories were true, a shameless womaniser. But he had risked his life for her cause and helped her save Ruthia. He might, she decided as she pocketed the box and turned toward *Fortune's Caress*, be worth her time.

*

The southerly winds brought with them new warmth,

and Akke breathed in the salty air as she watched the bow of *Fortune's Caress* cut through the deep blue waters. Behind her, the usual shouts and calls of a sailing ship's crew reassured her that all was well. Her body still ached when she moved in any way, and her healing skin itched against the fabric of her clothes. Her wounds had not been worth the expense of magical healing; given time, they'd heal on their own, and Akke had certainly endured much worse.

Her fingers traced the jewelled pendant hanging around her neck, and her eyes were drawn down once again to admire it. That scoundrel had underplayed things beautifully, she thought with a smirk, giving no indication of the value of his "token." Akke let her fingers dance across the fine craftsmanship of the necklace, recognizing the irony. Trying to steal a jewelled necklace years ago had forced her to flee Newport, and now another jewelled necklace beckoned her to stay.

Newport was a vile and disgusting city, but she was glad she'd come back. Ruthia was safe, and she had made a new … friend.

"Your guests are all sleeping peacefully," came a deep voice behind her. "All but one."

She turned, knowing that feline voice anywhere.

Ailuros looked a mess. His torso was still bandaged, having suffered multiple broken ribs, but his ragged fur was already starting to grow back thanks to Costa's potions of healing. Mostly concealed behind him, Ruthia's small form hovered an arm's length away from his swaying tail. She kept one wary eye on the panthor and one on the bustle of the ship around her.

"Well, I guess it's a start," Akke said.

"A princely gift," Ailuros said, admiring her new necklace.

"An effort by Costa to convince me that Newport isn't all bad."

"A very impressive man," he said, "for a human."

She simply nodded, not trusting herself to answer.

They all stood together in silence as the waves sloshed against the bow beneath them. Ruthia kept glancing surreptitiously over her shoulder at the sailors, her tightly bound hair threatening to come free in the wind. "Your Captain Regwald doesn't seem too thrilled at having us as new passengers," she finally ventured.

Nor would the Network appreciate this unexpected burden on their Fairhaven operations. But anything was negotiable, Akke had come to realize, and she had a lot to offer in exchange. She was already thinking about how to present her idea to Regwald to frame it like she was doing the Network a favour.

"He'll see that I'm right, in time."

Ailuros' throaty chuckle affirmed his opinion of her methods.

A sudden gust of wind caught her from the side, bringing a surge of warm, salty air. It made her think of the southern lands where that slaver had been bound. It was a big world out there, much bigger than even she'd seen, and having allies would serve her well.

"So, what do you plan to do with us?" Ruthia asked it casually, but her fists were clenched around the fabric of her worn skirt.

"Well . . ." Akke paused, wanting to tread carefully. "I've been gifted a tavern in Fairhaven. It hasn't opened yet, meaning I'll need staff for it. I'd like to offer you work there. Kitchens, cleaning, that sort of thing. You remember I said I work for ... some merchants?"

Akke would tell Ruthia about the Network given time. But for now, she needed to handle the girls with care. They had just traded service with one gang, and she wanted to ensure that in their minds, their new life in Fairhaven would be different.

And it would be, she promised herself. None of these girls would be abused or forced to serve the Network against their will.

Ruthia nodded.

"Well, the tavern will act as a ... meeting place, so they can attend to their concerns in privacy. It's important that they have a place to conduct their business safe from prying eyes, even sometimes from employees of the tavern."

"We can be loyal," Ruthia assured her. "All but Jayde have been part of a gang. And we'll make sure she knows what's what." Ruthia rubbed her ribs absently, and Akke felt a surge of protectiveness, remembered her own street beatings.

She paused, thinking. "And maybe," she added, "I can teach you all how to fight, and how to notice things."

"Your own assassin academy," Ailuros rumbled, nodding in approval. "I like it."

Ruthia's eyes went wide, her mouth dropping open to stare at the panthor.

"No!" Akke slapped Ailuros' shoulder gently. "Just enough so that they can stay out of trouble and defend themselves if necessary."

She turned her attention back to Ruthia. "He's joking. Really. But you should go lie down. Even if you can't sleep, think it over, and talk to the others when they wake."

Ruthia nodded, and tottered away along the deck, too nimble to stumble, but not yet used to the roll of the waves.

Ailuros shrugged. "I think my idea has merit."

Akke laughed and wrapped her arms gently around him. Surprised, he hesitated, then wrapped his around her. She pressed close to his strong, furry form, careful of his wounds, and gazed out to the open sea.

Ailuros, sensing her mood, purred, "He is a worthy companion, Akke, and you will see him again."

There was no hint of his usual banter. Ailuros approved of Costa.

"Thank you for helping me save those girls," she said. "I couldn't have done it without you. And I'm sorry your visit to my birthplace wasn't as much fun as you'd hoped."

"Are you jesting?" he retorted. "That was the best visit to any city I've ever had! This Newport is a wild, wretched, and wondrous place—we *need* to come again, witch."

She laughed again, hugging him a little tighter. "You're an idiot."

Thank you for reading Broken Promises

I hope you enjoyed it as much as I enjoyed writing it. I would like to take a moment to encourage you to share your thoughts by leaving a review on Amazon and/or Goodreads.

Your feedback would be greatly appreciated.

Please follow this link: Broken Promises, to be directed to the book's Amazon product page to leave an honest review.

Your reviews are important to me.

You can also join my non-spam mailing list by visiting my website.

Subscribers receive free content including short stories within the Fateful Force Series.

https://thefatefulforce.com/the-tome-of-syyx/

Thank you again,

Stavros Saristavros

Explore the World of Neptos, the home of The Fateful Force at www.thefatefulforce.com See other books in the series, access free D&D resources such as battle maps and a token maker for your own campaigns, or join us in our blog discussions on RPG gaming.

GROUPS

For fans of GameLit books, head over to Gamelit Society on Facebook, for all the latest news and releases in the genre.

ABOUT THE AUTHOR

Stavros Saristavros is a Greek-Australian world-building extraordinaire who creates elaborate fantasy realms based on his vast experience as a Dungeons & Dragons Dungeon Master.

When he's not enthralling his readers and D&D party members with his twisting plots and surprising character development, he shares free role playing game (RPG) battle maps and resources on his website for tabletop gamers, www.thefatefulforce.com.

As an avid MMA fan, he trains extensively in boxing, Brazilian Jiu-Jitsu, and is a black belt in karate—all of which helps him write realistic fight sequences in his action-packed novels.